FEARLESS
IN
HIGH HEELS

a High Heels mystery

GEMMA HALLIDAY

For my BFF, Jax.
Thanks for being my shoulder to cry on, my party pal to celebrate with, and my cheerleader always.

CHAPTER ONE

———

I watched as the dark figure moved through the forest. Mist swirled at his feet, the glow of the full moon above casting shadows across his beautifully sculpted face, his black hair curling over his ears in the damp night air as he stalked his prey. She stood, unsuspecting, on the other side of the clearing. A dark-haired woman, her back to him, her slim, pale neck exposed to the chilling night.

He spotted her. Then he smiled, showing off a pair of sharp, white fangs against his full lips.

I sucked in a breath, pulling my feet up to my chest.

Then I watched in horror as, in an instant, he was hurtling through the darkness toward the woman.

I covered my eyes with both hands. "I can't look. He's gonna bite her, isn't he?"

Dana sighed next to me. "Yes. Again."

I pulled my Snuggie up over my head. "Tell me when it's over." I burrowed into the pillows on my sofa where my best friend, Dana, and I were indulging in chocolate covered popcorn and hot cocoa while watching *Moonlight*, last summer's biggest blockbuster movie. I'd read all the *Moonlight* books but had made myself wait to see the movie until I'd finished the last one in the series. Which, as of this morning, I had. And I had to admit, it was worth the wait. The actress playing Lila was totally convincing as the naïve teenager who inadvertently falls in love with a local vampire.

Dana shifted beside me. "God, I hate this part, Maddie," she whined.

I peeked over the edge of my pink Snuggie at the screen. Lila was falling into the arms of her vampire would-be lover, Daniel, as his lips gently grazed her neck.

"Know what? I don't think he's biting her. I think it's just a kiss," I pointed out.

"Yeah, that's the problem." Dana crunched down hard on a piece of chocolate covered popcorn. Which was a sure sign she was upset. Dana never ate chocolate. Ever. Her body was a temple that ran on wheat grass, tofu, and mass amounts of exercise. She'd worked as an aerobics instructor, a Pilates instructor and a CrossFit trainer. Chocolate was to Dana was like garlic to Daniel and Lila.

"You okay?" I asked.

"Peachy. I love watching my boyfriend kiss other women," she said, heavy on the sarcasm.

"Sorry." I put a hand on her arm. "But you know it's just acting, right?"

Dana didn't answer, instead grabbing another handful of popcorn.

While I was caught up in the fantasy of the *Moonlight* world, Dana was stuck in the reality of it. Namely the fact that the sexy vampire currently caressing Lila's neck was actually Ricky Montgomery, Dana's boyfriend of the last two and a half years. While Ricky was no stranger to Hollywood, having begun his career as the hunky gardener on TV's prime time soap, *Magnolia Lane*, "Daniel" was the biggest part he'd landed yet, the *Moonlight* phenomenon launching him from TV hottie to teen idol overnight. Something Dana was not overly thrilled with. Not only had reviewers commented numerous times on the undeniable chemistry between Daniel and Lila - who was actually played by Ava Martinez, the sultry new member of the young Hollywood elite - but the last time Dana had gone to Starbucks with Ricky, no less than three women had asked Ricky to sign their boobs.

Not that Dana had anything to worry about, as far as I could tell. She was herself now an actress slash model slash Lover Girl cosmetics spokeswoman (her latest gig) who was blonde, stacked, and toned from head to toe. If Barbie ever needed a body double, Dana was your gal.

But I guess even Barbie might have issues with watching Ken smooch another girl.

"I don't get all this vampire fascination," Dana mumbled, crossing her arms over her chest and scowling at the screen as Daniel sunk his teeth into Lila, giving her "the eternal kiss" of night.

"You're kidding, right?" I responded, looking away as I grabbed a handful of popcorn. "Are we watching the same movie? Vampires are sexy."

"What's so sexy about drinking blood?"

I paused. Okay, she had me there. "It's not the blood thing," I countered. "It's that they're mysterious. Dark. Forbidden. The ultimate bad boys. Besides," I said gesturing at the screen, "you have to admit that Ricky looks hot in pale make-up."

Dana sighed. "Yeah. I know. Too hot."

"You know, there are worse things in the world than dating the guy every woman in America is lusting over," I teased her.

She threw a piece of popcorn at me, but smiled at least. "Well, with any luck, after he finishes shooting the sequel there won't be any more *Moonlight* movies."

"Aww," I whined before I could stop myself. "Why not?"

"Ricky's invested in this new club, and if it does well he said he'll be able to slow down a bit with the acting. Which," she clarified, "means more time with moi and less time with *her*."

"Tell me about the club," I said to cover my disappointment at losing my new favorite film series.

Dana perked up, crossing her legs under her on the sofa. "It's called Crush, and it's got this totally chic little spot on Sunset. Apparently Ricky's business manager suggested investing in it, so Ricky's now something like a one-sixteenth owner. I'm going to check it out tomorrow night. Oh! You should totally come with!"

I bit my lip. "Me? At a nightclub?" Okay, a few months ago, I would have jumped at the chance to check out a hot new club from the cushy VIP section reserved for one-sixteenth owners. As a fashion designer, people-watching among Hollywood's nightlife was one of my favorite hobbies. Some of my best inspirations had come from the dance floors of L.A.'s most fashionable clubs.

But recently something had come along to change all that. Okay, I guess you could say two somethings.

Number one: My husband, Detective Jack Ramirez, L.A.P.D. homicide. He was tall, broad shouldered, and built with all solid muscle. His hair was dark and always a week past needing a cut, his skin was a warm honey color year round, and his eyes were a soft brown when they crinkled with laughter at the corners and a deep, rich chocolate when he was in the mood for something a little more naughty. When a girl had a guy like that at home, what did she want to go out for?

And clearly we'd been spending a lot of time "in" together as I now had a reason number two to stay home: The Bump. In about twenty-two weeks I was told that said growth would actually become a living breathing human, but at the moment, it was just The Bump, a basketball shaped growth under my favorite T-shirt. (Which, even though it was stretched to the max I refused to give up in favor of the tents that passed as maternity clothes. Whoever said that maternity wear was "so much cuter" now than in the past clearly had a very loose interpretation of the word "cute".)

My first reaction to the two little lines on the pee stick had been surprise, then elation, then horror at the idea I was soon to be responsible for an entire life. Horror had settled into a dull sense of panic that I could most of the time smother with chocolate covered popcorn and hot cocoa, but it was still bubbling just below the surface enough that a nightclub wasn't high on my list of to-do's lately.

Dana must have seen the hesitation in my eyes as she looked down at The Bump too.

"Come on, it would be good for you to get out," she said.

"I don't know. It sounds like a normal person thing not a pregnant person thing."

Dana shot me a look. "You *are* a normal person."

"I'm a whale."

"You're not *that* big."

My turn to shoot the look. "I appreciate your dishonestly for my benefit, but I have mirrors. I know how big I am."

Dana waved me off. "No one will notice. It's dark in clubs."

"It's also loud. What if it's too loud for her?"

"Her?" Dana asked, jumping on the word. "Do we know The Bump's a girl?"

I shrugged. "Well, not technically. It's too early to know for sure yet. But I saw this to-die-for pink tutu onesie the other day at Macy's, so I'm hopeful."

"Well, either way, I'm pretty sure that thing can't hear yet," Dana said, staring down at my belly.

"She might be able to. I read in *What to Expect When You're Expecting* that she has ears now."

"Even if she does, the layer of fat will insulate her."

"See, you are calling me fat!"

Dana swatted me on the arm. "Look, if Crush gets too loud or too crowded or too anything, we can leave. But please come with me. It will be no fun without you." Dana pouted and batted her eyelashes at me.

The effect was so comical that I couldn't help the spurt of laughter that escaped me. "Okay, fine. I'll drag my whale-sized self to a nightclub just for you."

"Yay!" Dana said, bouncing up and down on the sofa cushion. "Trust me, we'll have a blast. It'll be like our last little club night before The Bump arrives."

"Hmm," I said, grabbing another handful of popcorn to cover the mild panic that always accompanied imagining my world post-Bump.

"'K, so I just have one more teeny, tiny favor to ask," Dana said.

I rolled my eyes. "What now?"

She glanced at the screen where "Daniel" was tongue kissing the newly vampireized Lila. "Any chance we could watch something else? *Anything* else?"

CHAPTER TWO

———

The next night found me ditching my Snuggie for the first time in months and letting my sofa fend for itself as Dana drove me through the packed Hollywood streets in her brand new convertible Mustang. Cherry red. With the top down. I had to admit, I was digging this last hurrah already.

Crush was located on Sunset Boulevard between Highland and Vine, in a black, square building set between a posh Italian restaurant and a women's boutique that specialized in pumps in size 11 and up. A single blue neon sign above the door was the only indication anything interesting lay within. That is, if you didn't count the line of women in tiny skirts and guys in skinny jeans spanning the side of the building, hopefully eyeing the door. Guarding the unassuming entrance stood a guy who looked like a heavyweight champ, a pair of black sunglass over his eyes despite the absence of sunlight.

Luckily, being that Dana and her plus one were on the list, we marched straight to the front of the line and were let in immediately. I thanked the gods for small favors. My shoes were already starting to bite into my feet as we entered the noisy room. In all honesty four-inch, pale pink, patent leather pumps probably weren't the most practical choice for when With Bump, but, my like my fav T, they were on the list of things I was not willing to give up, pain or no pain. Especially this pair. They were part of my new spring collection I was calling "Heaven in Heels."

The entire collection was done in soft, ethereal colors, and I was just three shoes away from completing it. With any luck, they would be walking the runways in New York in a matter weeks, and hitting exclusive boutiques everywhere in just a few short months.

At Dana's suggestion, I had matched my Maddie originals with a pair of cropped, black stretch pants and a long sequined tank that used to be a dress, but with the basketball protruding from my mid-section, was now more of a long shirt. But the overall effect was sparkly and cute, and if you saw me from the back, you could hardly tell I'd put on fifteen pounds.

Dana, on the other hand, looked like she'd come right from the set of one of her Lover Girl cosmetics shoots. She was in a tight, red mini-dress and tall, spikey red heels, and she wore a pair of silver earrings that dangled all the way down to her shoulders. I sighed watching heads (both male and female) turn her way as we entered the club. Oh, to be slim, hot, and un-bloated again.

"Isn't this place great?" Dana yelled to me above the pounding bass.

I nodded. "Great," I agreed, meaning it.

The interior of the club more than made up for the lackluster exterior. Plush red velvet lined the walls, pairing with shiny chrome fixtures and pendant lights. One large glass bar sat in the center of the room, packed two and three deep as people jockeyed to get the attention of the dozen bartenders in tight black shirts behind it. A pair of staircases snaked along the two opposite walls, leading up to a second floor where a DJ was playing music at top volume, spinning remixes of pop songs while bright blue, red, and green lights flashed across a crowded dance floor.

I had to admit, it looked like Ricky's financial advisor was a good one. The place was packed. On the dance floor dozens of wanna-be starlets crushed up against each other as VIP's looked on from private booths lining the walls. I could only imagine how much Ricky was making off this place, even if he was only making it off one-sixteenth of it.

"Let's get a drink," Dana said, grabbing me by the hand and threading her way to the far side of the bar where there seemed to be a small gap in the crowd waiting for drinks. After a minimum of elbowing, we finally made it to the front.

"What can I get you ladies?" yelled a bartender that was pierced in about fifteen different places. That I could see.

"Pom-tini," Dana yelled back over the noise.

"And a cranberry juice," I reluctantly added, really thinking a Pom-tini fit the atmosphere perfectly.

He nodded, then grabbed a couple of glasses.

"Excuse me," I heard behind me.

I swiveled to find a girl with long dark hair wearing a lot of eye make-up and very little dress, scowling at me. Her feet were encased in black, satin pumps with heels that ended in deadly looking silver spikes, making her tower over my 5'1½" frame. Behind her a redhead in an equally tiny dress, hers with a fashionable one-shoulder strap, and equally high heels did an equally ugly mirror image of the scowl thing.

"I'm trying to get a drink, here?" Dark-haired Girl said, her voice doing a bored-slash-annoyed thing.

"Sorry," I mumbled, trying to shimmy to the left a bit in the tight space. "I'm just waiting for my cranberry juice."

The girl did an exaggerated sigh, throwing her long hair over one pale shoulder, and she and her friend tried to squeeze past me. Which was a losing battle. The bar was packed with bodies, and there was nowhere left for me to get out of the way.

"I'm sorry, it's just really busy here-" I started.

But the girl ignored me, turning to her friend. And even through the crowded club I could hear her pseudo whisper, "Freaking whale's blocking the whole bar."

I froze, feeling steam gather between my ears. "What did you just say?"

"What?" she asked, blinking at me in mock innocence.

"Did you just call me a whale?"

"Did I?" she asked, still playing dumb.

"Yes. You called me a whale."

She shrugged. "Well, you're taking up way too much room, and you're not even drinking," she said, waving a manicured finger at me. "That is, like, way not cool."

"Uh oh," I vaguely heard Dana say beside me. But my full being was focused on Skinny Bitch Chick at the moment.

I clenched my teeth together. "For your information, I *am* drinking. A cranberry juice. So there."

She rolled her eyes at me. "Whatever, Shamu."

For a full second the world turned red, my face was filled with lava, and my tongue got stuck somewhere between my throat and my toes.

"*What* did you just call me," I hissed through my teeth, feeling all three tons of my weight clenching for a fight.

"Maddie," I heard Dana behind me. I felt her hand on my arm, tugging me in the opposite direction. "Honey, let's just go."

"I think this stick figure just called me a whale," I said. "I'm gonna kill her. I'm gonna sit on her. I'll suffocate her," I yelled even as I felt Dana drag me away from the bar. "How do you like that, Stick Figure? Ever been suffocated by a whale before?!"

Skinny Bitch Chick just shrugged again, sent me a look that said I was clearly the pathetic one, and slipped her emaciated little self toward the bar.

"You okay?" Dana asked, handing me my cranberry juice.

"Did you hear her? Did you hear what she called me?"

Dana nodded. "She's a twit. Ignore it."

Easy for her to say. She was still a size two. I sipped at my cranberry juice, willing the cool drink to cool me down even as I watched the Skinny Bitch walk triumphantly away from the bar, a red and blue cocktail in one hand and her equally smug sidekick a step behind.

"Come on," Dana said, watching my eye line nervously. "She's not worth spoiling our evening over. Let's go dance."

Normally The Bump and dancing don't mix well, but considering the anger still seething through me, I had some extra energy to burn off, so I let Dana lead me up a flight of stairs to the main dance floor.

* * *

As with downstairs, up on the dance floor it felt like everyone in Hollywood was at Crush. At least everyone who was anyone. We spotted a couple of Kardashians drinking in the corner, a couple of Disney Channel faux-teens dancing near the DJ, and a couple of current *Dancing with the Stars* contestants trying to tango to a Madonna re-mix. And along with Hollywood's elite were a few non-elite's that Dana and I recognized as well. Namely a slim, Hispanic guy in zebra printed, vinyl Daisy-Dukes and a red mesh tank with a boy toy in one hand and a martini in the other.

He waved the moment he saw us, wiggling his plastic clad butt our way. "Maddie, dahling, what are you doing here?" he gasped in an accent that was 50% Valley Girl and 50% San Francisco.

Marco worked as the receptionist at my step-father, Fernando's, salon while cultivating his budding career as a party planner. He was known for wearing more eyeliner than Lady Gaga, owning more pairs of leather pants than any other man (or woman) on the west coast, and having enough drama-queen in him to single handedly keep Broadway in business for the next decade. His current look included dying his hair bright yellow and drawing in a large, black beauty mark on his cheek, just above the cheekbone.

I greeted him with a couple of air kisses, before answering his question. "Dana's boyfriend is a part owner of the place."

"Fabu, honey!" Marco exclaimed, giving Dana a shoulder bump before he turned back to me. "But what I meant was what are *you* doing *here*? You know... in your *condition*?" he asked, pseudo whispering the last word as if saying it out loud might suddenly make pregnancy a catching disease.

"I'm having a good time," I hissed.

He scrunched up his nose. "Is that allowed when you're... you know?"

"I'm pregnant, not dead," I shot back.

Marco threw his hands up in surrender. "Okay, geeze, sorry for asking." He turned to Dana. "The hormones are making her a little touchy, no?"

"Who's your friend?" Dana asked, wisely changing the subject lest she need to pull the hormonal woman off another unsuspecting skinny person that night.

Marco's face brightened up immediately. "This," he said gesturing to the boy toy, "is Gunnar."

Gunnar was tall, blonde, tanned, and built like he'd just escaped from the set of *Baywatch*.

"Nice to meet you," Dana said.

Gunnar flashed a bright white smile at her and nodded.

"Gunnar's Norwegian," Marco said. "He doesn't speak a word of English. Isn't that precious?"

Gunnar smiled and nodded again.

I nodded back and did a universal "hello" wave. "He doesn't understand any English either?" I asked.

Marco shook his head, beaming. "None. He's an exchange student staying with your mom and Fernando," Marco explained. "They asked me to show him around. Some days, I love my job." He sighed, eyeing Gunnar's biceps.

"Well, it's nice to meet you, Gunnar," I told his blank expression. "But I think I have to go find the ladies' room. Cranberry juice overload."

Dana looked down at my glass. "But you only took a couple sips."

My turn to sigh. "I know. Peeing has become my hobby lately. You dance, I'll catch up to you," I told her, heading back toward the stairs.

It took a good twenty minutes to shove back through the crowded club again before I finally reached a door near the back with a little blue stick figure in a dress pasted on it signaling my Mecca. I quickly pushed through, instantly assaulted by the scents of hairspray, body spray, and something else that was lightly less aromatic. Three young, annoyingly slim, and fashionably dressed so-used-to-be-me women stood at the mirror primping, while two stalls sat behind them. Even in here the noise from the DJ was still deafening as I bent down and tilted my head under the stall doors, trying to peek for tell-tale feet. Just my luck, a pair of stilettos stared back at me under the first door. Next to a pair of loafers. I heard a moan from behind the metal door and it didn't take much imagination to realize what was going on in there. I think I blushed as I moved on to the second stall, and did a repeat.

Again, shoes. This time black, satin with tall, metal spiked heels. Great. Bitch Chick was in the second stall. Just my luck.

I crossed my legs, leaned against the hand dryer, and waited. And waited.

And waited.

Three minutes into it, I thought I was going to explode.

"Um, you going to be long in there?" I called out.

No response.

"There's a pregnant woman out here about to burst," I warned.

Again, nothing.

I moved to bang on the door with my fist, but the second my hand made contact, the door swung open.

And that's when, for the first time in five months, peeing dropped to number two on my priority list.

Sitting inside the stall, slumped backward on the toilet seat was the dark-haired girl I'd had words with earlier. And while she wasn't doing what one might think a person in a toilet stall would be doing, it was clear she was not going to be getting up any time soon. Her head lulled to one side, a trickle of blood dripped down the front of her dress, and her eyes stared at the ceiling, wide and unseeing. And totally dead.

CHAPTER THREE

———

Had the music not been so loud, it's possible I might have heard myself scream. As it was, the first sign I had that I was freaking out was a wave of nausea and a swaying of the room in front of my eyes. I blinked, took in a deep breath, willed my stomach contents to stay put as I grabbed onto the side of the stall, then took another deep breath.

Once I was pretty sure I remembered the mechanics of breathing again, I tried to force some logical thought into my brain.

Here's the thing: I'm ashamed to admit this is not the first dead body that I've found. Through no fault of my own, I seem to be some kind of dead person magnet. In fact, that's how I originally met my husband, the homicide detective. I'd like to think it's just bad luck on my part, but the truth is my dead-body-finding luck is beyond bad. It's downright disastrous.

I gingerly reached into the stall and put one finger to the side of Bitch Chick's neck to feel for a pulse. Her skin was still warm but had a distinctly rubbery feel that gave me a serious case of the heebie-jeebies. Not surprisingly, no blood pulsed there.

I pulled my hand back and instinctively wiped it on the seat of my pants to get rid of the dead person cooties. Yep, she was definitely gone. I mentally debated between calling the cops and grabbing the attention of one of the burly security guys Crush had roaming the floor. Considering calling the cops probably entailed lots of hanging out in the bathroom with a dead woman while on hold with 911, I went with option two.

I shut the stall door, said a silent prayer that no one else stumbled in here in the next two minutes, and backed out of the restroom.

The strobe lights and lasers from the dance floor immediately assaulted my eyes as I scanned the crowd for one of the guys in a black t-shirts with "security" printed on the back. I finally found one near a grouping of tables to the right and shoved my way through the crowds toward him.

"Dead girl," I panted as I reached his side, realizing I was out of breath.

The security guy squinted down at me. He was at least a foot taller than I was, at least a hundred pounds heavier (which was saying something, given my current condition), and his skin was two shades darker. He had intimidating bad-ass written all over him.

"What are you talking about, girl?" he asked.

I paused, took in a deep breath, willed my heart to slow down a couple of hundred beats per minute. "In the women's restroom. There's a dead body."

"You high?" he asked, his eyes narrowing further as he checked my pupils.

I shook my head so hard blonde hair whipped my cheeks. "No. I swear. Go look. She's really dead," I managed in a choppy breath.

He stared at me for another beat, still not convinced I was for real. Then finally said, "Show me."

While going back in there was the last thing I wanted to do, I was left with little choice. So I did, leading him toward the restroom. There was still a crush of girls primping at the mirrors, though thankfully Pumps and Loafers had finished their business, leaving one stall empty. I pointed with a noticeably shaky hand at the other one.

"In there," I said, hating how high and squeaky my voice was.

Security Guy knocked on the stall door. But, just as it had for me, it swung open before anyone could respond. Not that anyone in there *could* respond. I gulped back a wave of nausea again, looking away.

Security Guy was silent for a moment, his face unreadable as he stared into the stall. Then he finally said, "Oh yeah. She's definitely dead."

*   *   *

Forty minutes later I had finally relieved myself (in the men's room), the strobe lights were off, the lasers gone, the DJ's station silent, and the crowd assembled in hushed groups of three and four as uniformed officers questioned potential witnesses. Including yours truly. Dana, Marco, the silent Gunnar and I were all slumped in a booth near the back, awaiting round two of questions as officers huddled near the door to the ladies' room, whispering, pointing, calling in higher ranking detectives to do the dirty work.

One of whom I unfortunately recognized immediately.

"Uh oh," Dana said her eyes honing in on him as she voiced my thoughts exactly. "Isn't that..."

"Yep." I gulped down a ball of dread.

"You know what?" Marco said, spotting him too. "I think I'm just gonna go use the little boys' room..." he trailed off, sliding out of the booth, Dana and Gunnar a quick step behind him.

Traitors. Though, as I watched the reason for their quick getaway spot me, scowl, then make purposeful strides toward my booth, I kinda didn't blame them. I'd flee if I could, too.

He was tall and built like a boxer – all tight muscle and tough attitude. A faint scar ran through his left eyebrow, a black panther tattoo snaked down his left bicep, and his eyes were a deep, dark brown, so intense they were almost black as they bore down on me.

I cleared my throat and did a little one finger wave his direction. "Hi, honey."

My husband did not wave back. No smile, no hint of amusement whatsoever. In his defense, I guess finding your wife at your crime scene wasn't every detective's dream. But, in *my* defense, you'd think he'd be used to it by now.

I cleared my throat again and shifted nervously in my seat.

Ramirez crossed his arms over his chest. He looked from me to the yellow tape being stretched across the ladies' room door. Back to me. Then he slowly shook his head.

"Lucy, you got some 'splainin' to do. *Again.*"

I gulped. No kidding.

"Look, it wasn't my fault," I protested. "I just had to pee."

"You always have to pee. You don't *always* find dead bodies."

"I'd like you to remember that statement in the future."

He shot me a dark look. "Just tell me what happened, Springer."

Ouch. Last name. He was serious. I shifted again, then spilled it in the best so-not-my-fault way I could, telling him how I'd encountered Skinny Bitch Chick in the ladies' room.

When I was done he gave me a long, hard stare. "What on earth possessed you to take our unborn baby to a club in the first place?" he finally said.

I blinked at him. "Excuse me, last time I checked this was still *my* body."

"Carrying *our* baby."

"Well for another four months she goes where I go, and if I want to go to a club, I'm going. Besides, it's a club not a shooting range. What danger could she possibly be in?"

"Besides his mother getting in an altercation with a woman just before she's murdered?"

I bit my lip. "Oh. You heard about that, huh?"

He nodded. "Oh yeah. I heard. Apparently witnesses said you threatened to kill her? To suffocate her to death?"

"She called me fat!" I protested.

Ramirez closed his eyes. He did a silent two count, and I could see him employing a couple of those deep Lamaze breaths I'd been learning.

"Let's get back to the body," he finally said, opening his eyes again. "You said you found her in the restroom, correct?"

I nodded. "She was in a stall."

"Who else was in the restroom at the time?" he asked.

I scrunched my nose up, trying to remember specifics. "There were some girls in front of the mirror, but they were just hanging out there. And there was a couple getting busy in the stall next door."

The corner of Ramirez's lip quirked up. "'Getting busy'?"

I felt myself blush. "Doing… you know. Anyway, no, I didn't see anyone fleeing the scene with a knife in hand." I paused. "Or a gun?" I asked, realizing I wasn't exactly sure how Bitch Chick had met her demise. Admittedly, I hadn't done a thorough examination of the body in the stall.

Ramirez shook his head. "No evidence of a gunshot so far."

"How did she die then?" I asked.

Ramirez looked past me to the crime scene. "We'll have to wait for the M.E.'s report to be sure. But it looks like exsanguination."

"She bled to death?" I clarified.

Ramirez nodded.

I felt a frown pull between my brows. "But there didn't seem to be *that* much blood," I pointed out, remembering the thin trickle I'd seen earlier. "I mean, I saw a little on her dress, but not much."

He nodded. "I know. We're looking into it. It's possible she was killed elsewhere then dumped here."

I felt my frown deepen. Sure, that might have been possible… but only half an hour earlier she'd been at the bar insulting me. That didn't leave a lot of time for the killer to rush her somewhere else, bleed her to death, then rush her body back.

"What makes you think she bled to death?" I asked, wondering if maybe their theory had some holes in it.

Ramirez pursed his lips. "There were lacerations on her neck."

"Lacerations?" I asked. "Like, cuts? Stab wounds?"

He frowned. "Sort of. More like puncture wounds."

I narrowed my eyes at him. "Puncture wounds. On her neck. How many?"

Ramirez cleared his throat. "Two of them."

"Wait," I said, holding up a hand. "Are you telling me that she has bite marks on her neck?"

Ramirez's mouth took on a pinched look. "*Puncture* wounds."

"Holy shazbah, she was killed by a vampire bite?"

Ramirez shot me a look. "That's it. No more *Moonlight* for you, Springer."

"But you just said she was drained of blood."

"She bled out. I didn't say she was drained."

"And she had bite marks."

"*Puncture* wounds. And beyond that, I'm waiting for the M.E.'s report before speculating further on how or why the marks are on her neck. And," he added giving me a stern look, "I suggest you not speculate either."

Right. Only, how could I not? Pale skin, long black hair, bite marks, and death by blood sucking. It all added up to one thing as far as I was concerned.

Death by vampire.

* * *

"No way! Skinny Bitch Chick was a vampire?" Marco gaped at me across my kitchen table the next morning, almost spilling his mug of coffee.

I shifted in my seat. "I'm not sure we should continue calling her that now that she's dead. And, no, she wasn't a vampire, she was *bitten* by a vampire."

"Lord have mercy, this is the most exciting thing that has ever happened to me," Marco said. "Real life *Moonlight* hotties walking among us." He practically drooled at the thought.

Dana scoffed. "Come on. You don't really believe the vampire thing, do you?"

Marco shrugged. "A boy can dream," he answered.

I shook my head. "No, I don't really believe there are vampires roaming among us. But here's the thing: even if there is no such thing as a vampire, someone clearly tried to make it *look* like she was bitten by a vampire. Bite marks, blood drained. Someone either thinks they are a vampire or wants us to think they are."

"What do we know about Bit-" Marco paused, catching himself just in time. "About the victim?" he amended.

"Her name is Alexa Weston," I supplied, rattling off the stats I'd dragged out of Ramirez last night. "She's twenty-four, lives in Burbank, no record."

"You just described half the women in this town," Marco pointed out, sipping at his cup. Then he made a face, scrunching his nose and pursing his lips. "Honey, what is this stuff?" he asked me.

"Um, coffee?" I answered.

"You call this coffee? Mads, my baby bottle had stronger stuff than this in it."

"Sorry. I'm not supposed to have caffeine because of…" I gestured down to The Bump.

"So the rest of us have to suffer, too?" Marco whined, pushing his cup away.

"Well I just hope," Dana jumped in, "that Ramirez finds the killer - immortal or otherwise," she said shooting a look Marco's way, "quickly, and this can all just go away. Do you know what this has done to Crush?"

I shook my head.

"Ricky told me that they're closed until further notice. They're losing money like crazy every day that the doors are closed. Not only that, but a club closes down for a week in this town, and no one will remember it again."

Marco waved her off. "Sure they will. Someone was *killed* there."

"Great. I can only imagine what that will do to sales."

"It's Hollywood, honey. Every vampire wanna-be in town is going to be flocking to it hoping to get the bite," he argued.

Dana shot him a look. "Or it will go under because no investors will have anything to do with it, and there goes Ricky's slowing down. He'll be out of town filming more *Moonlight* movies." She grimaced. "With Ava."

"Come on. She can't be that bad," I jumped in.

"She posed nude for *Playboy* last week."

"I stand corrected."

Dana pouted again.

"Well, then we just need to make sure this case gets solved quickly," Marco decided, patting Dana sympathetically on the arm.

"I'm sure Ramirez is on it," I said. In fact, he'd been so on it that he'd come home only to change clothes and slip back out into the night again. A fact that had left me mildly disappointed, as I'd kinda hoped we could do a little under-the-covers making up after the not-so-fabulous encounter at Crush. Unfortunately, as I well knew when Ramirez had a case, he had a one track mind. Sleep, food, and wife fell out of the equation faster than you could say "homicide."

But Marco shook his head. "Sure, he's all over the fingerprints and DNA and witnesses. But what about the vampire angle? Is Ramirez really investigating that?"

I bit my lip. Not likely. In fact, he seemed pretty defiant that there was no angle. "I'm not sure he's really convinced about the vampire thing…"

"Right," Marco said. "But you said so yourself that someone went through some trouble to make it look like a vampire death. I'd say that makes it a pretty relevant angle."

I had to admit, I agreed.

"And who better," Marco went on, "to track down a vampire killer than us? I mean, how many times have you seen *Moonlight*?"

"Seven," I admitted. "This week."

He turned to Dana. "You?"

"Way too many," she answered rolling her eyes.

"I rest my case," Marco said. "We are totally vampire experts."

"Well, I guess it wouldn't hurt to ask a few questions…" I hedged.

Famous last words.

Marco squealed and clapped his hands. "Ohmigod, I've got the perfect pink trench coat for vampire slaying. I've always wanted to go Buffy all over some evil undead hottie!"

I rolled my eyes. I hoped for all our sakes that Ramirez was making more headway.

CHAPTER FOUR

———

Marco made himself a cup of real coffee while I took a shower, did a quick blow dry, mascara swipe and lipgloss application. Then I tried to wedge myself into a cute pink top and my favorite pair of jeans. Which almost fit. If I looped a rubber band through the button hole and around the button. But the top was a no-go. My belly stuck out beneath the hem like a giant white bowling ball. I conceded defeat and grabbed a long, skinny-tank to layer beneath it. Then I thrust my feet into a pair of sequined wedges from my summer collection.

"Okay, so where do we start?" I asked as we all piled into Dana's red Mustang.

"Um, duh, clearly looking for a vampire," Marco said.

I resisted the urge to roll my eyes at him from the backseat.

"Hey, are you rolling your eyes at me?"

Okay, I *almost* resisted. "Look, we can't just roam the streets looking for some guy with fangs. We need a real plan."

"Well, what about the friend?" Dana asked. "The girl Alexa was at Crush with. I think we should talk to her."

I nodded. "Perfect. Let's go back to Crush. Maybe someone there knows who she is and where we can find her."

* * *

Hollywood was quieter at this time of day, mostly filled with tourists and sightseers as opposed to the club crowd from yesterday. The outside of Crush looked a lot less interesting in the daylight – the steel grey door a nondescript opening, the sign above it dark, though the door was unlocked as we pushed through it.

While the swarm of police officers was gone, a few crime scene techs still lingered, dusting down tables and doorframes for fingerprints. I hated to break it to them, but they were going to find about a million of them on every surface. If this was the process of elimination the cops were employing, I had to agree with Marco that we had a fighting shot at catching the killer first.

To the right, the glass bar looked duller and decidedly more sticky than it had last night, a lone bartender standing behind it drying glasses with a white towel. He looked up as we approached, and I recognized him as the guy who'd poured our drinks the night before.

"We're closed," he said, spotting us.

"I know. We were actually hoping to ask you a couple questions," Dana responded, putting her elbows up on the bar.

The guy raised an eyebrow at her. "And you are?"

"Dana Dashel," Dana said, extending a hand across the bar to him. "My boyfriend, Ricky Montgomery is a part owner in this place."

The bartender looked from Dana's hand to her, then back at the hand. "Darwin Watts. But we're still closed."

"We were in here last night?" I jumped in, hoping to jog his memory into more friendly territory.

His gaze pinged to me, then narrowed.

"Yeah. I remember you. Cranberry juice."

"Right" I said, pointing to The Bump. "Anyway, we're looking into the death of Alexa Weston," I supplied.

Then added, "For the owners." Or at least one-sixteenth of them.

Up went his eyebrows again, his gaze going from Dana to me to Marco (who had, in fact, insisted on stopping by his place for a pink trench coat, a leopard printed fedora, and a black turtleneck that covered his entire neck from collarbone to chin, "just in case"), clearly not totally believing that anyone would trust an investigation to a pregnant lady, a blond in a miniskirt, and gay-lock Holmes.

"Was Alexa a regular here?" Dana asked, pressing forward.

The bartender shrugged. "I wouldn't say regular."

"But she had been in before?" I asked, jumping on that tidbit of info.

He shrugged again, turning his back to us as he grabbed another glass that was clearly already clean and started polishing away. "Sure."

"Sure?"

"I've seen her in once or twice before, I guess."

"What about her friend?"

He gave me a blank look.

"The girl she was with last night? The redhead? Had you seen her before?"

He shrugged again. "Sorry. A lot of people come through here every night."

I pursed my lips. This was getting us nowhere fast. "Do you know how she paid?" I asked, changing tactics. If we had the redhead's credit card receipt, we'd at least have a name.

Predictably he shook his head. "Dude, how am I supposed to remember how every patron pays?"

"What if I could tell you the drink she ordered?" I asked. "Could you look up if anyone paid with a credit card for that specific drink last night?"

He looked from Dana to me. "You sure Ricky Montgomery's your boyfriend? 'Cause I thought I saw him in here with Ava Martinez last week."

Dana's jaw clenched, her eyes narrowed, her lips curling into a thin line.

Uh oh.

"Look, if you could just do a quick check, we'll be out of your hair," I said, eyeing Dana's cheeks as they turned from sun-kissed peach to practically purple.

"That no good, home wrecking, little slut bag of a-"

"Easy, girl," Marco said, putting an arm around her shoulders. "I'm sure it was just a friendly drink after work thing."

Darwin looked from Dana to Marco, then back to me again, his desire to get rid of us suddenly overwhelming his aversion to questions.

"Fine. I'll check," he said turning to the register behind him. "But we sold hundreds of drinks last night."

"She was drinking a Cosmo with a lime twist and two cherries," I said.

Marco shot me a look. "Wow, you're observant, girlfriend."

"I've been drinking weak decaf and herbal tea for five months. I'm living my party life vicariously."

The bartender turned back to the register, scanning over the charges made last night. "Okay, Cosmo narrows it down to two hundred."

"You have a list of names?"

He shot me a look. "Look, even if she's sleeping with one of the owners," he said, gesturing to Dana, "that doesn't give you clearance to all the receipts. I could lose my job if I showed you this."

"Okay how about this: any of them on the same ticket as a martini with blue at the bottom, red on top, a maraschino cherry floating in it?" I asked, remembering Alexa's drink.

Darwin looked back at his screen. "That would be our special Blue Blood Baby. And, yeah. There is one credit card charge with both."

The three of us leaned forward.

"Name?" I asked.

"Sebastian Black."

I felt my nose scrunch up. "Sebastian?" Unfortunately that didn't seem to fit our mysterious friend.

"Maybe Daddy's footing the bill?" Dana suggested.

"Or a sugar daddy?" Marco supplied.

I nodded. It was possible. Both girls had been young, pretty, possibly pampered. "You have an address to go with that name, by any chance?" I asked Darwin.

He nodded. "Give me a minute and I can get it," he said, pressing buttons on the computer screen. Finally he grabbed a pen and jotted it down on a piece of receipt paper before handing it across the bar to Dana.

I looked over her shoulder. "Gardenia Way? Where's that?" I asked.

"Let's go find out," Dana answered.

We thanked the bartender, and five minutes later we were in the Mustang again, firing up Dana's GPS. Gardenia Way, as it turned out, was located in the Hollywood Hills, just off Laurel Canyon. And, twenty minutes and one pee stop at a Coffee Bean later, we were snaking our way up into the hills. On a winding road. A very winding road.

I couldn't help a small moan escaping me.

"You okay?" Marco asked, looking at me in the rearview mirror.

"I think I'm gonna be sick," I said.

"Lean out the window."

"Right. Fresh air is good."

Dana frowned at me in the mirror. "It is. And if the fresh air doesn't do it, can you kinda lean forward to do your business?"

"Your sympathy for my condition is overwhelming."

"Sorry. But I just got this thing detailed."

As crappy as I felt, I leaned, feeling like a dog out for a joy ride as I stuck my head into the wind.

I'm happy to say that by the time we reached Gardenia, I had managed to keep breakfast down. Though my hair was a windblown mess. I sighed in relief, doing a quick pat-down on my bangs as we pulled up to the address on the receipt.

"Whoa," Dana said, turning into a long driveway paved in sleek grey pavers. "This place is massive."

She was right. As the trees parted ahead of us, a wide, brick structure appeared. Wood beams crisscrossed over the façade, and two massive turrets rose up on either end of the building before it gave way to both east and west wings flanking the property. An oversized mahogany door with ornate carvings stood in the center, a stone carving of a raven hovering over it just below the eaves. It was a cross between California Spanish style architecture and a gothic fairy tale.

Dana pulled to a stop just to the right of the building. "Clearly our Daddy slash Sugar Daddy has money," she said as we got out and clomped up the stone walkway.

I agreed, wondering which stick figure it was that had belonged to this place – the dead girl or the friend.

I knocked on the wooden door, hearing the sound echo through the interior. We waited a couple of beats before the sound of footsteps on the other side indicated we'd been heard.

The door swung open and we were greeted by a guy that was tall, well over six feet, dressed in a pair of black slacks with crisp pleats and a white dress shirt. Though the shirt was un-tucked, the top two buttons open, and his feet were bare as if we'd either caught him getting dressed or in the middle of unwinding from a long night.

But my gaze was quickly torn from his clothing choice. Because as he opened his mouth to ask, "May I help you?" two smooth, sharp fangs shone brightly below his upper lip.

CHAPTER FIVE

I blinked, hardly hearing what he was saying, my eyes fixated on the fangs staring back at me. I repeat… fangs. Two tiny punctures wounds in Alexa's neck, two pointy teeth staring back at me. What were the chances they were unrelated?

Dana must have seen the same thing as she elbowed me in the ribs. "Dude," she whispered.

My thoughts exactly.

"Uh, I'm sorry, what?" I asked, forcing my attention away from the guy's teeth as I vaguely registered him talking to us.

He smiled, showing off the possible murder weapons again. "I asked how I could help you?"

"Oh. Right. Um, yeah." I cleared my throat, trying to focus on anything but teeth. "Uh, we're looking for Sebastian Black."

"You found him," he informed me.

"Oh." I'll admit, I was surprised. He was hardly the Daddy figure I'd been envisioning. Or the sugar daddy for that matter.

While the fangs had clearly been the attention suckers up front, I paused to take in the rest of him. He had jet black hair, cropped close to his head and gelled into a mass of tiny spikes that gave off a dangerous and oddly alluring vibe. While the vampire stereotype was pale skin, his was warmly colored to a California tan. In contrast to his dark looks, his eyes were a pale, brilliant blue, staring out at me beneath lashes that were long enough to make a make-up model jealous. His hands were shoved in his pockets, his demeanor the type of relaxed calm that only people who lived in multi-million dollar homes without mortgages could afford.

"So," he said, as I silently studied him, "was there something you wanted of me?" He punctuated the prompt with a smile. I wished he'd stop doing that. It was eerily distracting.

Get a grip, they're just fangs. I cleared my throat again and forced myself to focus on our reason for being here.

"We're looking into the death of Alexa Weston," I said.

The smile faded instantly from his face. "You're police officers?" he asked, his gaze flicking momentarily to Marco's fedora.

Dana shook her head beside me. "Not exactly. We're affiliated with Crush. The nightclub where she died?"

Sebastian nodded. "I see."

"You knew Alexa?" I asked.

Again he nodded. "Perhaps you'd better come in."

I hesitated. Wasn't accepting an invitation to a vampire's house one of those things that meant he could suck your blood? Or was it inviting one into your house? Damn, it had been too long since I'd watched *Lost Boys*.

Reluctantly, I stepped over the threshold of the open door as Sebastian held it open, feeling Dana and Marco do the same behind me.

While the outside of the home may have resembled an old-world villa, the interior of the house was all modern Hollywood. Clean lines, sleek furnishings in organic materials, and a muted color palate. The floors were a cool, white marble, the walls a soft beige, and the artwork hanging in all directions done in large scale black and white photos of abstract architectural shapes. The overall effect was clean and crisp, yet with just enough touch of warmth to be inviting.

We followed as Sebastian led us into a room to the right where a pair of low, modern sofas in plush chenille and a pair of arm chairs sat beside an enormous window overlooking the valley. Sebastian sank into one of the chairs. "Please, have a seat," he instructed, motioning to the sofa.

I did, perching on the edge, a little afraid that I might not be able to get up if The Bump and I sank too far in.

"Tell us about Alexa," Dana said, jumping right in as she sat down next to me.

Sebastian lifted the corner of his mouth ever so slightly. But instead of answering turned to me and said, "I'm sorry, I didn't catch your name?"

I cleared my throat, (a third time, for anyone who was counting), unnerved under his icy blue gaze. "Maddie. Maddie Springer. And these are my friends, Dana and Marco," I said gesturing beside me.

But Sebastian's level eyes never left mine. "Very pleased to meet you, Maddie."

Why the sound of his voice running over my name should send a chill up my spine, I had no idea. But the way the word rolled off his tongue was slow, soft and almost sensual. I found myself shifting in my seat, suddenly as fidgety as a five-year-old.

"Now that the introductions are taken care of, want to answer the question?" Dana pressed.

Sebastian's eyes lingered on me just a moment too long before slowly turning to my friend. "What do you want to know about Alexa?"

"For starters, what is your relationship to Alexa?"

"Alexa was an employee of mine," he answered.

"In what capacity?" Dana asked.

"She was an actress."

"So, you're a producer?" I asked.

Confusion must have been clear in my voice as he turned to me with that half smile pulling at his lips again. "Of sorts. I produce events. Parties, I supposed you could call them. Specialty parties for a special set of clientele."

"That's very vague," I pointed out.

Sebastian's smile bloomed into a full fang-ed affair. "Yes. It is."

Again, I felt my inner kindergartener shifting uncomfortably.

"What kind of parties are we talking here?" Dana asked.

"Oh," Marco said piping up. "Are they…" he leaned in, stage whispering, "sex parties?"

Sebastian shook his head, amusement lighting his pale eyes. "No. Fantasy parties."

"Like, vampire fantasies?" I asked, the pieces falling into place as I eyed the teeth again.

He nodded. "Yes."

"What goes on at these parties?" Marco asked, his eyes glinting with a light that said he was fishing for an invitation.

Sebastian cocked his head at Marco, answering slowly. "The usual. Dining, dancing, drinking."

"Drinking…?" I let the question hang in the air.

He smiled at me, a lopsided thing ripe with amusement. "*Cocktails.* Like I said, the parties are fantasies. They're an escape from the everyday. A chance to live in a different world, if only for one evening. A world where the fantasy of immortality reigns. Everyone stays young, and there is no death, no disease. No hangovers," he added winking at me.

"And there are people willing to pay for this fantasy?" Dana asked.

"Oh, yes," he answered. "You'd be surprised at the guest lists. Doctors, lawyers, politicians. The people who live the most mundane, upstanding lives are the ones with the richest cravings for escape."

His eyes went to me on that last note, lips curling into a half smile again that hinted at some sort of shared secret.

I shifted in my seat, studiously looking away.

"And Alexa worked at these parties as what?" I asked, steering the conversation back to our purpose for being here.

"As a vampire, of course."

Of course.

"So it's all make believe," I said (watching Marco's shoulders slump with disappointment out of the corner of my eye). "The fangs are fake?" I said.

Sebastian's eyes leveled on me again. "Mine? No, these are real."

I paused. I wasn't sure if this guy was putting me on or putting himself on.

"When was the last time you saw Alexa?" Dana jumped in.

Sebastian sat back in his chair, a small frown marring his otherwise smooth features. Incredibly smooth, I noticed. Suddenly I wondered how old he was. His demeanor would have me putting him somewhere close to my own early thirties, possibly older, but unless he was using some really amazing night cream the absence of lines on his face spoke to someone much younger.

"Alexa worked a private party for me two nights ago," he answered. "That was the last time I saw her."

"Did she leave alone?" I asked.

Sebastian paused, and I could see him carefully formulating his answer. "My actresses always leave alone. What they do once they leave here, I have no idea. That's beyond my control as an employer."

I raised an eyebrow. Why did I get the feeling he was being purposefully vague again?

"Did Alexa have any enemies?" Marco cut in. "Anyone who would want her dead?"

Sebastian shook his head. "Not that I know of. Then again I wasn't on personal terms with her. She was an employee."

"How long had she worked for you?" Dana asked.

"A few weeks."

"And how deep into the vampire fantasy was she?" I asked.

He shrugged. "She was very good at her job. Beyond that, I can't tell you what her preferences were, whether or not she chose to live the lifestyle outside of work."

Whether she chose to live it or not, it had certainly been a part of her death. Which brought me to my next question…

"What do you know about sanguinarians?" I asked, pulling the term from my *Moonlight* education.

Sebastian turned to me, the twinkle of amusement shining in his unnaturally pale eyes again. "You mean drinking blood?" he asked.

I nodded. "Yes."

"Okay, I'll bite." He paused, then grinned. "No pun intended," he added with a wink. "Sanguinarian is the technical term for a person who has an inherent thirst or physical need, that lies outside of eroticism or fetish, to drink blood. Los Angeles has the largest recorded number of sanguinarians in the United States. According to the 2010 census more than two-hundred and seventy-five thousand of them reside in southern California. Is that what you wanted to know?"

I bit my lip. And slowly nodded. Though I noticed he the use of the world "them" to describe the blood drinkers and not "we". I wondered if it was intentional or a slip of the tongue.

"Was Alexa involved with anyone at your parties who was a sanguinarian?" I asked.

Sebastian frowned. "May I ask why you'd like to know?"

"Because she was killed last night," Dana pointed out.

I could see thought churning behind Sebastian's eyes, but his face was impassive enough that I couldn't read them. "And this has to do with my parties because...?"

"She bled to death. From a pair of bite marks on her neck."

"Messy," he answered, his face still impassive.

"You'd think. But there actually wasn't much blood at the scene at all."

"So, what are you saying?"

"I'm saying that..." I paused. I wasn't really sure what I was saying. It seemed silly now that I was voicing our theory out loud.

"That a vampire bit her, drank her blood, and killed her," Marco finished for me, never one to worry about looking silly.

Sebastian looked from Marco to me to Dana, then back to me again. "And you're here to accuse me?"

"If the fangs fit," Marco said, with a lot more bravado than I currently felt, pinned to my seat by those intensely pale eyes.

But while I might have expected Sebastian to get defensive when being accused of sucking the life out of a person, he seemed as cool and calm as he had since we entered his modern lair.

"I'm sorry, but you're way off track," he told Marco.

"So point us to the right one," I offered. "Who might have done this to Alexa?"

He shook his head. "Like I said, I wasn't privy to her personal life."

"Do you know who might have been?" I asked. "She had a friend with her last night. A redhead?"

"Becca?" Sebastian asked.

Bingo. "Do you have a last name for Becca?"

"Diamond. She worked for me as well. Why?" he asked.

I hesitated to tell him that she was as of now suspect nurermo uno. "She may have been the last one to see Alexa alive."

Sebastian frowned. "That's troubling."

I'll say.

"So, Becca is one of your vampires, too?" Dana clarified.

"Actress. But, yes, she plays that role."

Maybe one Becca took too seriously. Had she fought with Alexa over something? Had she bitten her and – my stomach rolled at the thought – actually drained her friend of blood? "Do you know where we can find her?" I asked.

Sebastian nodded. "I can look up her personnel file. Excuse me for a movement." He got up and moved from the room.

As soon as the three of us were alone, Marco leaned forward. "Did you see how he floated out of here?"

"He didn't float. He walked. Gracefully," I added.

"Did anyone notice if he had a reflection as he walked past the artwork? Did you see him in the glass?"

I rolled my eyes. "He is *not* a vampire, Marco."

"Are you sure?"

"Yes!" Mostly.

Marco opened his mouth to argue, but before he could make another case for the undead, Sebastian returned, a slip of paper in hand.

"Here's the phone number and address we have on file for Becca," he said handing the paper to me. I cringed in anticipation of a cold, clammy hand but was met with normal flesh. I gave myself a mental shake. I'd been watching too much *Moonlight*.

"Thanks," I said, slipping it into my purse as I rose.

"I would appreciate it if you would keep me apprised of your findings," Sebastian said as he led us back toward the front door. "And please let me know if there's anything I can do to help."

I nodded, thanking him for his time, even though I had the distinct feeling that last offer was a hollow one.

Especially if he was the blood drinker we were after.

CHAPTER SIX

———

The first thing I did when we got back to the car was dial Becca's number. It rang seven times, then unfortunately went to voicemail, where I left her a message with my name and number, asking her if she could please call me back.

"So, what do we think of Fang?" Dana asked as I hung up.

That was a loaded question. I thought he was hiding something, for certain. But whether it was about Alexa's death or his own unique drinking problem, I wasn't sure. And adding to that uncertainty was the shiver still sitting mid-spine that his icy blue eyes had created. Dangerous, intense, seductive. Totally unnerving.

So instead I shrugged. "Question mark?"

"Good way of putting it," Marco said, nodding in the passenger seat. "You can never be sure what vampires are capable of."

Dana and I did a synchronized eye roll. "Seriously, Marco?" I said. "You can't really believe there are vampires among us?"

Marco blinked at me in the rearview mirror. "Hello? Did you not hear the man? There are two-hundred and seventy-five thousand real vampires among us."

"Two-hundred and seventy-five thousand *weirdoes* that *claim* to drink blood," Dana clarified.

"Po-tay-toe, po-tah-toe," he annunciated, waving me off. "I'm still glad I'm wearing a turtleneck, because that guy - Hey, did you guys just roll your eyes at me?"

* * *

After all that eye-rolling and vampire questioning, I'd worked up an appetite. Luckily, there was an In-N-Out Burger conveniently situated just off Laurel Canyon, after a minimum of whining on my part about my starving baby, Dana agreed to stop.

Marco ordered a protein burger – meat, lettuce, tomato, no bun – saying he was watching his carb intake now that he was seeing Gunnar. Dana ordered water, saying that everything on the menu was loaded with fat and non-organic pesticides. I ordered a double, double with extra cheese, a side of animal style fries and a Neapolitan shake, saying nothing.

Marco looked at my tray. Back up at me. Back to the tray, then down at The Bump.

"Hey, the burger and fries are for the baby," I explained. "I'm only eating the shake."

He shrugged. "Fair enough."

Once we'd fully consumed our lunch (me and Marco making little yummy sounds throughout and Dana making little disgusted sounds throughout), I stopped for a quick pee break, then we were back in Dana's mustang.

I tried dialing Becca's number again, but again got voicemail. This time I didn't leave a message. Instead, I plugged the address into Dana's GPS and we hit the freeway.

The address on the paper Sebastian had given us was just off Sunset, east of the 101. While Sunset Boulevard in Hollywood proper was full of souvenir stands and tourist stops, the east side was full of crumbling apartment buildings and trash can fires. The architecture here was mid-century modern meets eighties crack house, the glamorous homes of the semi-famous from Hollywood's heyday having deteriorated into tenements that now housed rats the size of purse-dogs. If this is where Becca was living, it was clear that the vampire gig wasn't a big money maker.

Becca's building was a square block of concrete set between an adult film shop and a liquor store having a sale on Marlborough cartons. We circled the block, then found a spot on the street two buildings down. Dana beeped the car alarm twice, just for good measure, and said a small prayer that her baby would still be there when we got back, before following Marco and me into the lobby of Becca's building.

The floor was a cracked linoleum, the walls a dull grey, and the scent a mix of urine and Chinese take-out. A set of stairs sat to the right and an elevator to the left. Unfortunately, the elevator held a cardboard sign with the words "Out of order" written across it in sharpie. Fab.

"What floor does Becca live on?" I asked, eyeing the stairs versus my wedges.

Dana checked the paper again. "Unit Four-seventeen."

Fourth floor. Sigh.

"Okay, let's get this over with," I huffed, taking the first flight just a step behind Dana and Marco.

By flight number two, I was feeling the burden of carrying fifteen extra pounds. By flight number three, I was getting winded. By flight number four, I felt like a hippo was sitting on my chest, and I was carrying hundred pound barbells on my shoulders.

"I (pant) hate (pant) stairs (pant, pant)."

"You okay?" Dana asked, concern puckering her brow.

"You're not gonna drop a baby on us here. Are you?" Marco asked, panic in his eyes.

I shook my head. "I'm fine. I just need (pant, pant) a second."

"I think it's just down here," Dana reassured me, indicating a hallway to our right filled with closed doors and painted-on numbers.

I did a couple of deep Lamaze breaths to slow my panting, then followed her until she stopped at four-seventeen, a unit at the end of the corridor near a garbage chute that reeked of diapers and rotting food. I quickly plugged my nose. It nature's cruel trick on the pregnant that just when you're the most queasy you've ever been in your life, your sense of smell suddenly goes into hyper drive, picking up every lovely nuance of scent.

Dana shot me another look. "You okay?"

"I'b fine," I said, sounding like I had the mother of all colds. "Let's do dis."

Dana nodded, knocking on the door. We waited, listening to silence on the other side. Nothing.

Dana knocked again, as I breathed heavily through my mouth, willing my gag reflex not to engage.

Again, no answer.

"Maybe she's not home," Dana suggested, putting an ear to the door to listen for sounds.

But I wasn't ready to give up that easily. I'd just climbed up four flights of stairs. I was not going home empty-handed. I knocked with my free hand, waited a two-count, then tried the door handle.

What do you know, it turned easily in my hand.

Dana and Marco both registered my own mix of surprise and concern on their faces. This was not a good sign. No one in this neighborhood would leave their front door unlocked. In fact, no one I knew in L.A. left the door unlocked at all – even when they were home.

I carefully pushed it open a crack.

"Hello?" I called out. "Becca?"

No one answered.

"Becca? Are you here?" I opened the door all the way, taking a tentative step into the room.

And froze.

The place was trashed. Sofa cushions tossed, tables upended, lamps knocked over, kitchen cupboard contents littered all over the floor.

Someone had clearly beaten us here.

CHAPTER SEVEN

———

"Becca?" I called out again, noting the panic edging into my voice.

I moved into the apartment, stepping over the mess as I heard Dana and Marco do the same behind me.

Marco whistled low. "Oh, honey, someone has done a number on this place."

No kidding.

The living room was small, roughly the size of my closet, with an equally doll-house sized kitchen attached at one end. A stove, refrigerator and oven took up the entire kitchen, looking rusted and worse for the wear above more ripped linoleum to match the lobby. Beyond the living space sat a doorway leading to what I guessed was a bedroom. I gingerly stepped over a couple of broken picture frames and sofa cushions toward it.

"Becca?" I called out again. "Are you here?" Though, honestly, I didn't expect an answer. If she was here, she clearly would have heard us in the shoebox apartment by now. But I found myself holding my breath anyway as I peeked my head around the doorframe.

As expected it was a bedroom, holding a twin bed and a scarred wooden dresser. Only the bed had been stripped of its linens, the contents left in a heap on the floor along with a couple of pillows that were molting down feathers from their busted seams. The dresser drawers were open, clothes spilling onto the floor.

"She in here?" Dana called, coming into the room behind me.

I shook my head. "No. It's empty." And so was, I noticed, her closet. The tiny cubby hole held a single wooden bar where only a couple of wire hangers sat. Someone had cleaned out Becca's belongings in a hurry.

"The bathroom is empty," Marco called, his head popping into the doorway. "And her make-up is gone, too."

Which all added up to one thing, I realized with a sinking sensation in my stomach: our number one suspect was MIA.

* * *

I arrived home to a note on the kitchen table saying Ramirez would be out late (bummer), but that his mother had brought over some enchiladas that were in the fridge. (yay!) I immediately pulled out a casserole dish that smelled like chilies, cumin, and cilantro and popped it into the microwave to reheat. A little sour cream and a mashed up avocado later, and I was in heaven. I was just going into a food orgasm when the doorbell trilled.

I reluctantly left my feast and opened the door to find my mom and step-dad on the other side.

"How's my grandbaby doing?" Mom asked my belly, immediately putting two hands on The Bump.

"I'm doing great. Thanks for asking."

Mom's eyes shot up to mine. "Oh. Sorry. I'm just so excited to meet him," she said, making little cutsie faces at my belly.

"How's our preggo princess feeling, dahling?" my step-dad asked from behind her. Ralph, or Faux Dad, as I'd affectingly dubbed him, was the owner of Fernando's Salon, believed unwaveringly in the uses of spray tans and Botox, and had shocked the entire world when he'd married my mom, dispelling everyone's beliefs that he was gay (mine included). While Faux Dad was what is generally referred to as a "character" in Beverly Hills, he was a sweet guy, made my mom happy, and gave me all the free pedicures I wanted. So I had to love the guy.

"I'm doing fine, Ralph, thanks," I answered.

"I'm so glad she's cooperating for you. Any morning sickness? How's the nausea? The cravings getting bad yet?" he asked all in one breath.

"Some. Good. No. What are you guys doing here?" I asked as they pushed into the room.

"We brought you a pre-sent," Mom said in a sing-songy voice, holding up a pastel yellow bag with little duckies printed on the side.

Well, presents weren't all bad.

"What is it?" I asked, peeking in over the tissue paper.

"Open it." She thrust it proudly toward me.

So, I did, tearing the tissue out and digging my hands inside.

I came out with a soft, vinyl doll in a little yellow onesie covered in more ducks.

I blinked. "What is this?"

"It's Baby-So-Lifelike."

I raised an eyebrow at her. "You do know I'm having a real baby soon, right?"

Faux Dad nodded beside her. "Yes, and that's why you need practice with Baby-So-Lifelike."

Mental forehead smack. "Guys, I'm not twelve. I don't need to play mommy with a doll."

"*Practice,* not play, dear," Mom corrected. "And, yes, you do. Honey, you have no idea what it's like to have a child."

"I'm sure we'll figure it out."

"It's my fault," she continued, running right over me. "I should have given you a little sibling, someone to look after."

"Mom, I think we'll manage-"

"Or at least a dog! I've left you completely unprepared for parenthood."

"No one is prepared for parenthood," I told her, repeating the reassuring words of my Lamaze teacher.

"Oh, I know, honey," Mom said. She cocked her head to the side and did a frown-slash-smile oozing with sympathy. "But you are particularly unprepared."

I rolled my eyes. "Gee, thanks."

"No, no, like I said, it's not your fault. And I don't mean to be unkind, but it's just… well, remember your ficus?"

I put my hand on my recently-ample hips. "Yes, I had a plant. Yes, it died. Plants die. That's not the same as a baby."

"And remember the replacement ficus I brought you?"

I paused. "Yes."

"And then remember the plastic ficus I brought you after the replacement ficus died?"

"Vaguely," I mumbled.

"What happened to that one?" she prompted.

I threw my hands up. "Okay, fine. I left it too close to the stove, and the plastic one melted. I can't even keep a plastic plant alive."

Mom handed Baby-So-Lifelike to me. "Keep him away from the stove, honey."

I looked down at its plastic blue eyes staring up at me, its chubby limbs outstretched.

God help me.

* * *

It was warm. So warm I was sweating, my clothes clinging to me like Saran Wrap. I wiggled, turning from one side to the other, sure I was melting from the inside out. But I couldn't get out of the tight clothes. I was going to suffocate in my own outfit.

Then suddenly I felt a hand on my shoulder, cool breath on my neck.

"Let me help," a soft male voice whispered in my ear. And he did, his hands on my arms, sliding the sleeves of my shirt low until my right shoulder was bare. It felt wonderful. Heavenly, as a cool breeze wafted over me, creating goosebumps.

Then he dipped his head low, his lips kissing their way across my exposed skin. A shiver snaked down my spine despite the heat still searing into me. Heat that was moving, changing, traveling south and ending just below my waist. Intensifying until a moan escaped me, and I wriggled closed to him. His body was solid, cool, his hands commanding, but it was his lips that I craved. His lips were so soft, so smooth, so feather light on my skin. Not warm, like you might imagine, but cool. Cold. Ice-cold and so welcomed against my over-heated skin. I was dying to feel those lips everywhere – my neck, my earlobes, my mouth. And then, as if he could read my thoughts, his kisses traveled higher, his breath dipping at the small of my neck as his lips whispered across my jugular. I moaned again, unable to help myself.

I turned my head to get a look at my husband.

But it wasn't Ramirez's face I saw.

The pale blue eyes staring back at me were Sebastian's, framed in impossibly long lashes below spiky black hair that clung to his head looking wild and dangerous. He grinned at me, slowly, wickedly, showing off a pair of gleaming white fangs, then swiftly dipped his lips to my neck…

I sat up with a gasp, my breath coming hard as I fought with the sweaty sheets tangled around my legs. I blinked in the darkness, trying to get my bearings. Slowly, familiar shapes came into focus. My cherry dresser, my mirrored nightstand, my closet, doors open and overflowing with shoeboxes.

I was in my own bed, in my own bedroom. It was just a dream. I let out a long breath, slowing my heart rate down. Just a dream.

Just a little, nothing to worry about, sex dream about a vampire.

I glanced over at the blinking numbers on the alarm clock. 1:13 AM. And, I noticed, no husband lying in the empty spot on the other side of the bed. I flipped on the bedside lamp and shoved my feet into a pair of fuzzy pink slippers, going in search of said husband.

A single light was on in the living room, next to the sofa where I could see Ramirez reading in the shadows. I had no idea when he'd gotten home, but a cup of coffee beside him told me he hadn't yet entertained the idea of sleep. He had a sheaf of papers in his hands, flipping through the pages. His face was in shadow, his cheeks dusted with stubble, his features softened by exhaustion just enough to give him a warm, inviting look. I felt a remaining tingle from my erotic dream hinting as I sat down beside him.

"Hey," I said softy.

He looked up, a grin quickly spreading across his face. "Hey, yourself. I didn't wake you, did I?"

I shook my head. "I couldn't sleep."

"Me neither," he sighed, staring down at the papers in his hands again.

I leaned in close, my head resting on his shoulder. I inhaled deeply the woodsy scent of his morning aftershave, still clinging faintly to his collar. And felt that tingle kick up a notch. "What's that?" I asked, pointing to the paperwork.

"Just work," he responded, throwing an arm around me.

I snuggled closer. "Work? The Alexa Weston case by any chance?" I asked.

He nodded. "Background reports."

I squinted down at the small type. "What's it say?"

"Not much, unfortunately. She grew up in San Diego, then moved north about three years ago to start an acting career."

"Family?" I asked.

"Parents are dead. She has one sister in Corona Del Mar."

"And?"

"And the local PD talked with her yesterday. She hasn't seen Alexa in months. Apparently Alexa was a bit of the family back sheep."

Imagine that.

"You get the medical examiner's report back yet?" I asked.

I felt Ramirez shift beside me. "No. And even if I had, I'm not sure I'd be sharing it as bedtime reading with my wife."

"Hey, I found her body," I protested.

"So what else is new?" he mumbled.

I gave him a playful elbow to the ribs.

"Ouch. Watch it," he said, but I felt his torso bob up and down with a suppressed chuckle.

"I'm just feeling a little guilty about it all," I confessed.

"Why? You kill her?" he teased

I gave him a less playful elbow this time.

"No. But I did wish her dead right before she turned up dead."

"Which had nothing to do with her *actual* death," Ramirez pointed out.

I nodded. "I know. But, well, I just feel bad. Had I known it was her last night on Earth, I might not have called her a bitch."

Ramirez hugged me tighter and planted a kiss on the top of my head. "I'm sure she's not holding it against you."

The kiss was nice. Comforting. And if it was a little lower and a little slower, it might turn into something else. "You coming to bed?" I asked, getting up.

Ramirez shook his head, picking up the papers again. "Soon. I just want to go over a couple more things here."

"Oh." I tried not to let my disappointment show. "Okay, 'night."

"'Night, Maddie. And, hey, don't worry," he added. "We'll catch whoever did this to Alexa."

I nodded. "I know," I said before shuffling back to the bedroom. Which was the truth.

I just didn't know which one of us would catch that person first.

CHAPTER EIGHT

"Seven a-m," I said with a sigh.

Dana blinked at me. "So?"

"Ramirez didn't come to bed until seven a-m," I told her and Marco over cups of herbal tea the next morning. A fact that had distressed me so much that as soon as Ramirez had slunk out of bed and slipped off to work that morning, I called Dana for a much needed girl-whine. Good friend that she is, she'd called Marco for back-up and they'd both shown up on my doorstep a scant fifteen minutes later with a box of tissues in one hand and a box of chamomile in the other.

"And he left me again at nine," I added.

"He didn't leave *you*. He left for *work*," Dana said, sounding way too logical.

I nodded. "I know. You're right. But you're missing the point. When he's at work, I can handle that. But he was *here* last night. He just didn't want to sleep with *me*."

"Honey, are sure you're not overreacting just a little?" Marco asked, sipping from his paper cup. He'd wisely stopped at Starbucks on the way here today, bringing with him a fully loaded latte. Vanilla if my nose didn't deceive me. With cinnamon. I was so jealous.

I shrugged. "Yes. No. I don't know. But this is the second night in a row that I've slept alone. And I just know that… well… things aren't the same lately."

"What things?" Dana asked.

"Very important things."

"Such as?"

I sighed. "Such as, do you know when the last time we had sex was?" I asked.

Marco shot a look at my belly. "I'm gonna say five months?"

"Ha. Ha. Very funny," I mumbled. Even though he was almost right. I'd like to think it was a coincidence that the homicide rate had suddenly picked up the same time I started looking like a large water mammal, but lately I was starting to have my doubts.

"I'm just not sure I do it for him anymore, you know?"

"He's just busy," Dana reassured me. "You know how he is when he's hot on a homicide. Ramirez is crazy about you. I mean, didn't he come home early last Monday?"

I nodded. "Because we had Lamaze class."

"Well, what about the week before. He took a whole afternoon off, didn't he?"

"To help me pick out a jogging stroller," I pointed out.

"Honey, your social life is making me sad," Marco said.

I shot him a look. "Watch it, pal. I outweigh you by a good twenty pounds at the moment."

Marco looked down at my belly again. But he shut up.

"Look, I'm sure when this case is wrapped up, Ramirez will be all over you again," Dana said.

"I don't know if I can wait that long," I whined. "I mean, you have no idea what it's like. I'm experiencing… well, some pregnancy side effects that I'm having a hard time dealing with on my own," I hedged.

"Like what?" Dana asked, concern drawing her eyebrows together. "Nausea?"

"Not today."

"Bloating?" Marco asked.

I shot him a look. "Do I look bloated to you?"

He was wise enough not to answer that.

"Pickle cravings?" Dana asked.

I shook my head. Even though a pickle didn't sound half bad, now that she mentioned it.

"Is it the gas?" Marco asked, scrunching up his nose. "I heard pregnant women have excessive gas."

"No! God, you guys are really making me feel better about myself here."

"Sorry," Marco mumbled, though his nose was still scrunched up as if he wasn't 100% convinced.

"So, what is it?" Dana asked.

I bit my lip. "It's, well, it's kind of embarrassing, but… it's the hormones.'

Dana gave me a blank look. "Like… weepy hormones?"

I shook my head. "Worse. Horny hormones."

Marco let out a blast of laughter, and Dana covered a snort with her hand.

"I'm serious!" I said. "The hormones running through me right now are insane. I'm like a fifteen-year-old boy or something. All I can think about is sex," I said, remembering my dream from last night all too vividly.

Marco giggled again, but Dana put a sympathetic hand on my arm. "I'm sure that as soon as Alexa's killer is caught, you can get Ramirez to set aside some alone time to… take care of your problem."

I nodded, sincerely hoping she was right. "Speaking of which, I got some background info on Alexa last night," I told them, quickly filling them in on the scant few items I'd picked up from Ramirez's reports.

When I'd finished, Dana said, "It doesn't sound like Alexa and her sister were particularly close."

I shook my head. "No. But one thing Ramirez said stuck with me last night. He said that her sister described Alexa as the family black sheep."

Marco nodded. "Being a vampire will do that."

"But Ramirez said that her sister hadn't seen her in months. Alexa only started the vampire gig a few weeks ago. So what made her the black sheep before then?"

"Oooo, good question," Dana agreed. "Maybe she was into some bad stuff before, and it caught up to her."

"What do you think it could have been?" Marco asked.

I shrugged. "I don't know. But I bet her sister does. Anyone up for a trip to the beach?"

* * *

Twenty minutes later I was showered, blow-dried, and stuffed into a pair of stretchy white pants, a flowy, oversized pink baby-doll top, and a pair of cute, suede ankle boots. I grabbed an oversized white, leather tote and met Dana and Marco at the curb beside her Mustang.

Marco took one look at my tote and scrunched his nose up. "What's that?" he asked.

I looked down. "What? It's a Santana. It's very this-season."

"Not the *bag*, Mads. The *arm* sticking out of it."

I looked down again. He was right. One chubby, vinyl arm was peeking over the edge of the tote. I quickly tucked it back inside.

"It's nothing," I mumbled.

"Maddie," Dana said, drawing out the word. "Should we be worried about you?"

I threw my hands up. "Fine. It's Baby-So-Lifelike, okay?"

"Baby so whatnow?" Marco asked.

"My mom thinks I need practice being a good parent, so she gave me this doll to lug around."

"Yeah, I'm not so sure good parents stuff their kids into their Santana bags," Marco informed me.

I shot him a look that could freeze his latte in two seconds flat. "Just get into the car, Auntie Marco."

* * *

Corona Del Mar, Spanish for "crown of the sea", is about an hour south of Los Angeles and actually a pocket of Newport Beach that's just expensive enough to get its own name. Dana had the address I'd swiped from Ramirez's background report last night programed into her GPS, and only two wrong turns later we pulled up to 712 Cambert Drive, home of Phoebe and Bill Blaise. It was a single story, typical California ranch style home on a street lined with palm trees. While we were a good two miles from the ocean, the air still had a salty tinge to it. I inhaled deeply, the sweet scent a welcome change from the perpetual ode de smog that had hung in the air over L.A. since our last big rain.

Dana parked the Mustang at the curb, then we walked up the front steps, where Marco gave a sharp rap on the door.

Two beats later it was opened by a tall man with a thick head of dark hair, thick glasses on his nose, and a thick, dimpled neck that looked like it was made of flesh-colored Play-Do. "May I help you?" he asked, his voice a deep baritone.

"We're looking for Phoebe Blaise?" I asked, trying to look past him into the home. From what I could see of the living room, light pine and nautical navy blue dominated the color scheme, large, comfortable looking furniture filling every nook and cranny.

"And may I ask who you are?" he said, suspicion lacing his voice as he took in our threesome.

"My name is Maddie Springer," I said, trying my best at authority. "And these are my colleagues. We're looking into the death of Alexa Weston."

"The police were already here," he hedged, his eyes going from Dana (today dressed in a black tube top, hot pink skirt, and matching hot pink wedges) to Marco (still donning his pink trench, though he'd paired it with leopard printed pants and a purple tank top today), to me and my baby-filled tote.

"We're not with the police," I quickly reassured him. "We represent the club where Alexa was killed."

He nodded, this seemingly a little easier to believe. "I'm sorry, but I'm not sure what help we can be."

"We were just wondering if we could ask Alexa's sister a couple of quick questions, then we'll be out of your hair," I promised.

While I could see reservation still marking his face, he nodded again. "If you make it short. She's very distressed by this whole thing."

"Of course," I agreed.

"I'm her husband, Bill," he offered, holding the door open for us. "Please, come in."

We did, following him through the nautical living room to the kitchen beyond, also done in a beachy theme. Seashells of every shape and size were glue-gunned onto coasters, canisters, and even the low chandelier above the whitewashed dining table. At the table sat a woman with short, blonde-from-a-box hair and dark eyebrows a week past a good threading. Her hands were wrapped protectively around a coffee mug, as if it was the one thing anchoring her to the room at the moment. I inhaled deeply the scents of fresh brewed French roast, unable to keep the wistful sigh from escaping me.

"Phoebe?" the man said softly, as we entered the room. "We have some visitors."

The woman looked up, and it was clear she'd been crying recently. Red rimmed her eyes, along with dark circles beneath.

"Yes?" she asked, looking from her husband to us.

"They're here to ask a few questions about Alexa," he told her. He sank into the chair beside her, gesturing for us to sit down as well.

"I'm Dana, and this is Maddie and Marco," Dana said. "We represent the investors in the nightclub where your sister was killed."

At the use of the word "killed", the woman cringed, her lips drawing into a tight line. The man put a hand on her shoulder in a comforting gesture.

"We're so sorry for your loss," I quickly jumped in.

She nodded, trying hard, I could tell, not to cry. "Thank you."

"And we're determined to see your sister's killer brought to justice," Marco added. "Which is why we were hoping we could ask you a few questions about Alexa?"

"Like we told the police, we haven't seen Alexa in months. I'm not sure what we can tell you about her," the husband repeated.

"When exactly was the last time you saw her?" Dana asked.

The woman frowned. "Summer, maybe? She drove down with a friend."

"Becca?" Dana asked.

Phoebe bit her lip, then shook her head. "I'm sorry, I really don't remember the friend's name."

"Can you describe her?"

"About Alexa's age, slim." She shook her head again. "They were only here for a few minutes. I don't think I even spoke to the women, to be honest."

"That's a short visit," I observed.

"They were always short," her husband broke in. "Alexa only drove down here for one reason: money."

Again, Phoebe's face took on a pinched look. "Alexa had some misfortune in her life. She needed help from time to time."

"More like all the time," her husband countered.

"Bill-"

"You know it's true," he said, his tone softer.

Tears welled up in the woman's eyes, but she didn't argue this time.

Her husband turned to us and continued. "Alexa had been chasing the Hollywood dream for years. Once in while she'd land a small part and could pay her own rent. Between those, she'd show up here with her hand out."

"But she was doing better lately," Phoebe cut in, defending her sister.

"How so?" I asked.

"A couple of weeks ago I called to see if she needed help with the rent," she said. "But she said she didn't. She said she was doing fine for money."

"Because she had a job?" I asked, thinking of her vampire gig.

Phoebe's eyebrows drew together, and she shook her head. "I don't know. It wasn't the impression that I got. She said she'd hit a windfall. That she expected to come into some real money soon."

Honestly? Phoebe was right. That didn't sound like the language someone would use to describe steady employment. But I still made a mental note to ask Sebastian just how well he paid his vampire hostesses.

"Did she say what sort of windfall?" I probed.

"Probably illegal," the husband piped up.

"Bill," his wife shushed him.

But I jumped on it, coming to the point of our being here. "Had Alexa been involved in illegal activities in the past?"

Phoebe bit her lip, her eyes shooting to the dregs left in her coffee cup.

But her husband bobbed his head up and down, vigorously. "You name it, Alexa got mixed up in it. When she was younger it was vandalism and loitering. Then it was drinking, shoplifting. No matter how many times we bailed her out of something, she'd fall right back in with the wrong kind of people, doing all the wrong things."

I suddenly wondered if one of those wrong people had killed her.

"But Alexa didn't have a record," I argued, remembering the clean slate Ramirez had told me about.

He nodded. "And we worked hard to make sure of that. In most cases, we paid restitution, and no one pressed charges." He glanced at Phoebe, drawing his lips into a tight line. "Look, for my wife's sake, I'm sorry that Alexa is gone. But honestly, I'm not surprised. It was only a matter of time before one of those people she hung out with turned on her."

But the question was, which one?

CHAPTER NINE

———

"I think it was Becca," Dana said as we munched on sandwiches at a shop two blocks from the sister's place. Mine a BLT with extra mayo and extra bacon on the softest sourdough I'd ever tasted. Marco's a lean turkey breast wrap with lettuce. And Dana's sprouts and egg white salad on a whole wheat roll that looked hard enough to make my nausea come back.

"Why Becca?" I asked, sipping at my soda.

"Well, it's a little suspicious that she's gone, no?" Marco added.

I nodded. "Yes." I paused. "Okay, what about this? Let's say that this windfall that Alexa came into was from something shady. You think Becca knew about it?"

Dana shrugged. "They were friends. I know I'd tell you about any windfall I got."

"Awe. Ditto, bestie," I said, doing a warm-fuzzy moment. "Okay, so let's say Alexa tells Becca about it."

"Or, better yet, let's say they were in on it together," Marco said, nodding as he munched.

"But maybe Becca gets greedy and wants it all for herself," I added.

"So she kills Alexa, grabs the cash, and takes off!" Dana finished.

I nodded. "We really need to find Becca. She's the key to all of this."

Dana paused, taking another bite of her health on a bun. "You know, I remember when I was just starting out in the acting business. No matter where I went or what I did, I always made sure that my agent could always get hold of me in case a role came up."

I raised an eyebrow her way. "You think Becca's agent knows where she is?"

"It's worth a try."

"And you can find out who that agent is?"

Dana grinned, showing off a sprout stuck between her molars. "Piece of cake. Give me ten minutes, and I'll have all her deets." She pulled her cell from her purse and began furiously texting.

Only *seven* minutes later we'd finished our sandwiches (plus a couple of cookies on my part), and Dana's phone buzzed to life with the answer we'd been looking for. According to Dana's former co-star's husband's best friend's manager, both Alexa and Becca were signed with the Bowman Agency in Encino.

One hour and two pee stops (I knew I shouldn't have ordered the large soda.) later, we pulled up to The Bowman Agency's offices located just off Ventura. It was a small storefront in a strip mall, sandwiched between a Mexican bakery and a nail salon advertising $20 acrylics. Not the most prestigious of addresses by a long shot.

And the inside wasn't much better, I noted as we pushed through a pair of glass doors. The furnishings were pure Craigslist – mismatched chairs, a coffee table in eighties black laminate, and a magazine rack that tilted slightly to the left. As the door shut behind us, a bell on a piece of orange yarn jangled above us, and a moment later a short, paunchy guy emerged from the back room. He had a full head of jet black hair, with just the hint of grey roots growing near the hairline, and his face was a weathered tan like he'd either spent too many hours at the pool or too many session under a tanning bed. He was dressed in a pair of pants that were tight enough to show off the shape of his wallet, ending in a pair of snakeskin cowboy boots. He'd kill it at a Johnny Cash look-alike competition.

"May I help you?" he asked, an eager light in his eyes as he took in Dana's short skirt, long legs, and obvious It quality.

"We're looking for Herbert Bowman?" Dana asked.

The man smiled, showing off a row of white veneers that were at least two sizes too big. "That's me! What can I do for you lovely ladies," he said, kind enough to make the compliment a plural even though I noticed his gaze had barely flickered to Marco or me.

"We're looking for Becca Diamond," Dana said.

"Oh." His smile faltered for a half a second. "Uh, are you interested in booking her? I can check on her availability."

I opened my mouth to set him straight, but Dana jumped in before I could.

"Yes! Yes, we are."

"Wonderful," Bowman said, clapping his hands. "Please, come into my office," he instructed, leading the way into the back room.

"We are?" I whispered as the three of us followed the agent.

"What better way to corner her?" she mumbled back.

I nodded. "Clever."

"Please, sit down," the faux Johnny Cash said, sinking into a leather office chair behind his desk as he indicated a couple of metal chairs with seventies inspired orange and avocado prints on the seat cushions.

"Thanks," I said, complying. The chair groaned under my weight, and I suddenly wasn't sure if the chairs were inspired or original.

"So what sort of job is it that you'd like to hire Becca for?" he asked.

"Uh…" I shot Dana a blank look.

"Music video," Dana supplied, lying seamlessly through her teeth. "See, I'm launching a music career, and I really need this first video to be fabulous."

"Love it, love it," Bowman said, his eyes shining with dollar signs. "Becca is an excellent dancer. And singer, if you need some backup."

"That's what we're counting on," Dana said, flashing him a big smile.

"I understand you represented Alexa Weston, too?" I jumped in.

At the name of his fallen client, his "on" face slipped, his eyes going moist for a moment. "I did. It's such a terrible tragedy what happened to her. What a waste of talent."

I murmured agreement and nodded. "Alexa and Becca where friends, right?" I asked.

Bowman nodded. "Yes. I often booked them together. But," he quickly added, "if you're looking for another girl, I have several clients who would be perfect to work with Becca on a music video."

Dana shook her head. "No, that's fine. We're just interested in Becca."

"When was the last time you saw Becca?" I asked.

Bowman paused. "Why?"

Oops, maybe too direct? "Uh, well, I just wanted to make sure that she still looks like the pictures we've seen." Hey, I was catching on to this lying game.

Bowman nodded slowly. "I can assure you that she would not change her style without letting me know."

"So, you've seen her recently?"

"I have. She was in here a couple of days ago and looked perfect. Camera ready," he assured me.

"A couple of days ago. That was before Alexa died," I noted.

He nodded. "Yes, they were both in. They were collecting their checks for a tampon commercial they did."

"How big were the checks?" I asked, remembering the mention of the windfall.

Bowman frowned. "I'm sorry, I don't think that's something I should share."

"What she means," Dana said, jumping in to save my horrible-liar butt again, "is that our production has a tight budget. We heard a rumor that Alexa and Becca were commanding higher pay lately, and we're quite frankly a little concerned that we may not be able to match them."

God, she was good. I nodded next to her like a bobble doll. "That's right. We're concerned."

Bowman pursed his lips, and I could see greed warring with the fear of losing a paying gig. Finally fear must have won out as he leaned forward, putting his elbows on the desk. "Look, to be honest, the commercial was a regional thing. I'd doubt the amount of the checks could pay their rent, let alone qualify as 'high pay,'" he said, doing air quotes with his fingers.

"Is it possible they've been working under the table somewhere else?" I pressed.

Bowman shook his head. "No way. I'd hear about it. I'm very well connected."

While his modest digs made me question the last part of that statement, I knew for a fact that Hollywood was a small world. Chances were he honestly would have gotten wind of them moonlighting eventually, especially if it was a high paying gig. And while Alexa and Becca may not have been brain surgeons, I had a feeling even they weren't stupid enough to risk it.

Which meant Alexa's windfall had to have come from somewhere else.

"So that means," Dana said, her own mental wheels turning beside me, "that you booked them for all their jobs. Even the vampire parties?"

Bowman scoffed. "Great, you've heard about those?"

"Oh, have we," Marco jumped in.

"Look, I told them not to do that job."

"Really?" I asked, leaning forward. "Why not?"

"It ruined their credibility. That Sebastian character may have some ridiculous stuff going on at that place, but I know the kinds of movers and shakers that are into ridiculous extra curricular activities. Alexa and Becca were more likely to run into a big name director at one of the parties than they were at the farmers' market. They were pigeon-holing themselves before they even got a part."

"But you booked them on it anyway?"

"In case you didn't notice, I'm not exactly repping Tom Cruise here," he argued, gesturing around his office. "I gave them my honest opinion, they ignored it, what can you do?" He shrugged.

"Did the parties pay well?"

Bowman shook his head. "Well below scale. Then again, they aren't exactly union jobs, if you know what I mean." He paused. "Look, you want to book Becca or not?" Bowman asked, some of the eagerness he'd originally displayed having been questioned out of him.

Dana nodded. "Definitely. As soon as possible."

"Great," Bowman said, turning to an ancient computer monitor beside him and squinting at the greenish font. "She's free all next week?" he offered.

"We were hoping for sooner," I said. "Like… today?"

"No can do," Bowman answered, shaking his head. "She's booked tonight."

"Where?" I asked, leaning in.

"One of those vampire parties at Sebastian's place. She's book from 10:00 PM on."

* * *

"I knew it all came back to vampires!" Marco stage-whispered, grabbing my arm as we left Bowman's.

"Okay," I conceded. "Let's say, just for kicks, that however Alexa came into her windfall is tied to the vampire parties."

"I bet it was Fangs," Dana said. "He looks loaded. I bet he was paying them to do something illegal."

"He did seem a little cagy about what happens after the parties," I agree. "Maybe he was paying the girls to sleep with his guests?"

"Hooker vampires? I love it!" Marco said, clapping his hands together. "Or, even better, maybe he was paying them to suck their blood!"

I shot him a look. "Gross."

"Hey, the body was drained of blood," he pointed out.

"True. But there was only one pair of bite marks on her neck. Meaning she was only drained *once*. If someone had been," I cringed, nausea creeping up on me again "drinking her blood on a regular basis, there'd have been older marks."

"Well, maybe it was a one-time thing? He paid her for one blood suck, but it got out of hand, and he sucked too much blood?"

"Can we not say the words 'blood' and 'suck' together anymore, please?" I pleaded, willing my stomach to sit still. "Besides, there's one problem with your theory."

"Only one," Dana mumbled as we got back in her car.

"What problem?" Marco asked, ignoring her.

"Why kill Alexa at the club? I mean, if Sebastian really did hire her for some sort of drinking thing, it stands to reason he'd do it in the privacy of his own home. Why risk doing it at a crowded club?"

Marco pouted. "Good point. Well, whatever Alexa was into, I'm betting both Sebastian and Becca are into it up to their fangs."

"So you guys think Becca will show up at Sebastian's party tonight?" I asked.

Dana turned to me, her eyes suddenly gleaming with a Cagney and Lacey look I knew all too well. Though in reality, we were probably closer to Lucy and Ethel. "Oh, Maddie. Are you thinking what I'm thinking?" she asked, a grin dimpling her cheeks.

"That a cheeseburger would really hit the spot right about now?"

"The party tonight! It's our one chance to corner Becca and grill her."

"I don't know…" I hedged. "Maybe we should just turn all this info over to Ramirez and let the police sort it out."

Marco scoffed. "Like the police could blend in at a vampire party."

"They don't have to blend, they have warrants," I countered.

"No, Marco's right," Dana argued. "We're much more likely to get info about Becca by going undercover than the police are by busting through the doors, badges drawn."

I bit my lip. She had a point.

And she could tell she was wearing me down. "Please, Maddie," Dana pleaded, clasping her hands together in front of her. "Ricky's *Moonlight* contract is up for renewal for a third movie next *week*. If the club is still closed by then, I just know he's gonna sign."

I let out a sigh. As much as I hated the idea of walking into a possible blood drinking orgy, I had to admit that this was our best, and possibly only, chance of catching up with Becca.

"Fine," I relented. "Let's go rent some fangs."

CHAPTER TEN

Luckily Dana knew the perfect place to get vampire attire – the set of *Moonlight II: The Eternal Kiss*, the sequel that half the known world was awaiting with baited breath (yours truly included) and which was currently being filmed at Sunset Studios in Hollywood.

Sunset Studios houses the biggest and best names in both television and film, and is encircled by an impenetrable wall that is so heavily guarded it makes Buckingham Palace look like a joke. Inside the paparazzi-proofed walls, the studio grounds are laid out like a small city; only the city is a little schizo. There are streets of Brooklyn brownstones butting up against suburban tree-lined neighborhoods, right next to a futuristic post-apocalyptic town that also doubles as the old west, depending on which production is currently shooting. Dana and I had once gone undercover to help in one of Ramirez's investigations here, and I'd gotten lost wandering the pseudo neighborhoods on more than one occasion.

Today, however, we did not need to go undercover as, thanks to Dana's movie star boyfriend, she was on The List. One look at her ID and the guard at the massive iron gates waved us through, indicating parking in a lot just to the right, where we quickly traded her Mustang out for a golf cart, the studio's main method of transport.

Moonlight II was being shot in the Brooklyn neighborhood, today, a rare daylight scene involving Lila and Daniel being forced to walk among mortals to find a magic potion that turns vampires into humans for just long enough for them to consummate their relationship. (A scene which Dana was not looking forward to. Rumor had it Ava had been paid extra to go full frontal.) We parked our cart on the edge of the set, then walked in, stepping between camera tracks, lighting racks, and microphone cords to a pair of white trailers set against the storefront of an Italian deli. "Ricky Montgomery" was taped to the door of the first in block letters, "Ava Martinez" on the other. Dana spared one dirty look at door number two before knocking on door number one.

A dirty look that, as it turns out, she could have delivered in person, as Ava opened the door to Ricky's trailer a beat later.

She blinked, batting long, fake eyelashes at us. "Yeah?" Ava asked, unceremoniously.

"We're here to see Ricky," Dana informed her.

"And you are?"

Dana's teeth gnashed together. "His *girlfriend*."

"Oh." Ava gave Dana slow up and down, doing a hot-girl-to-hot-girl assessment. "I see. Well, I guess you can come in then," she said, standing back to allow us entry.

I could tell it took all Dana had not to elbow the stick figure out the door as she passed by her. Very big of her, really.

I, on the other hand, actually *was* very big and did end up knocking into Ava in the tiny trailer doorway. Just a little.

"Sorry," I mumbled. "Bun in the oven."

"I can see that," Ava responded, eyes flickering to The Bump. "What's that in your bag?"

"Nothing. Just a baby."

She frowned and opened her mouth to respond, but never got the chance as Ricky emerged from the back room.

"What a surprise! What's my favorite gal doing here?" he asked, moving in to give Dana a peck on the cheek.

While Ricky's image on the big screen made moviegoers across the world swoon, I had to say that the in-person version was even more spectacular. He was tall – well over six feet – had broad shoulders, slim hips, and every inch of his body was hard muscle, attesting to his gym-rat status. His hair was black at the moment, long and lose to his shoulders. Which might have been a little too early-Banderas to be sexy had his skin not been tinted a pale white that was so ethereal, the entire look was kind of mesmerizing. I could see why girls were hot for him. I firmly gave my own over-active hormones a down-girl talk as I perched myself on the edge of his sofa.

Marco sighed beside me, echoing my own thoughts as he whispered, "God, that man is hot."

"Smokin'." I nodded, watching Dana return Ricky's hello with a kiss. I noticed that she included a little tongue for Ava's benefit.

"Wow, nice to see you too," Ricky said once she let him come up for air. "To what do I owe this surprise visit?"

"Can't a girl come visit her *boyfriend*?" Dana asked. Though whether she was talking to Ricky or Ava, I wasn't totally clear.

"If that's the kind of hello I get, you can visit any time," Ricky said, still grinning.

Dana shot Ava a look that said round one had clearly gone to her.

Ava narrowed her eyes. "Actually, Ricky and I were kind of in the middle of something, so maybe this isn't the best time."

"I'm sure it can wait," Dana shot back.

"I don't think so. It's very important."

"What could be that important?"

"We're rehearsing our next scene."

"Oh, which one?" I jumped in, unable to stop myself from going fan-girl just a little.

Ava smirked. "The one where Lila and Daniel have sex."

Dana froze, her entire body tensing.

Uh oh. I had to ask.

Dana turned to Ricky, her eyes narrowing into tiny slits. "You were *rehearsing* this scene?"

Ricky nodded. "We were just running lines when you got here."

"How many lines are there?" she hissed. "It's sex."

"Oh, you'd be surprised," Ricky said, cracking open a water bottle, seemingly completely oblivious to the steam starting to spout from Dana's ears. "It's way harder than you'd imagine to have sex on camera."

"*Pretend* to have sex on camera," Dana corrected, shooting daggers at Ava from her slitty eyes.

"Rwar, cat fight," Marco whispered.

"So anyway," I broke in, figuring we better get to the point of the visit before we had another dead body on our hands. "We were wondering if we could borrow a couple pairs of fangs for the night? We have a vampire party to go to and need something authentic."

Ricky nodded. "Totally. The ones they have in make-up are great. Glue on, stay put all day."

"Even through kissing scenes," Ava said, shooting a saccharine smile at Dana.

Dana's teeth clenched so tight I feared we'd need the jaw of life to pry those suckers open.

"You think we could impose on make-up for a few minutes?" I asked Ricky.

He shrugged. "Sure. Want me to show you where the trailer is?"

"Please," I urged, grabbing Dana by the arm and steering her out of the room before someone got hurt. Not that I would blame her. Ava was, as it turned out, a bit of a twit. But I honestly wanted to let the twit finish filming.

* * *

If Sebastian's estate had seemed fairytale-esque before, it was positively Gothic after dark. The turrets loomed against the evening sky, casting long, eerie shadows across the circular drive. The trees lining the estate were lit from below, creating long, silvering fingers up to their tops. And the bricks framing the front door took on a sinister red hue. As a stark contrast, the circular driveway was lined with shiny, modern cars tonight, all way pricier than my bank account could afford.

Dana parked her Mustang between a Jag and Ferrari and cut the engine. From here, we could already hear music radiating from inside, above a soft muffle of voices, a slow organ playing a song that belonged in a haunted house.

"Are we sure about this?" Marco piped up from the backseat. "I mean… maybe we should have brought some garlic or a wooden stake with us."

I rolled my eyes. "I think we'll be okay."

"You know, I pride myself on my flawless neck."

"Look, Sebastian said they're all fake anyway," Dana reassured him, swiveling in her seat.

"Sure. Right," Marco agreed, nodding. "Only one of those *fake* vampires sucked Alexa dry."

"Do you want to stay in the car?" I asked.

Marco nodded. "Yes, please."

"Fine." I shoved my leather tote at him. "Then you can babysit."

Marco opened his mouth to protest, but I hopped out of the car before he could, leaving the chicken-livered vamp in the backseat.

Honestly? I wasn't a whole lot of notches higher on the bravery scale. While I wasn't worried (much) about having my blood sucked, it was highly likely that we would encounter a murderer tonight. Not a comforting thought, no matter what kind of costumes we're talking.

I adjusted my fangs as we walked up to the massive front door, hoping we could blend well enough.

In addition to the teeth, the *Moonlight II* costume department had been gracious enough to let us raid their stock of extras' outfits for loaners. After we'd totally geeked out at the array of choices, Dana had finally settled on a long, corseted, black dress with a slit up the side showing off her legs. It sat just off the shoulders, so we paired it with a spider-web inspired shawl and a pair of fishnets that mimicked the pattern down her legs, ending in spiky red heels. I'd dittoed her fishnets, but I'd obviously had to forgo the corset. Instead, I'd found an empire waisted black velvet dress that was just long enough to cover The Bump, short enough to show off my lace-up boots, and wide enough that I could thankfully still fit my butt into it. And, to cap off our looks, we'd both donned long, black wigs borrowed from the hair trailer. Overall, we were feeling total vampire-chic as we slipped inside the heavy, mahogany doors of Sebastian's house.

Which looked as if Victorian London had suddenly collided with Miami Beach. Men and women in dark, drapey clothing mingled to the sounds of J Lo telling them to get on the floor from speakers hidden in the antique moldings in the ceilings. Large, opaque goblets circulated among the guests on trays held by women in mini-skits, dark stockings, and tight tops.

And everywhere that people laughed, smiled, or talked, fangs peeked from behind their painted lips. Seriously, fangs all over the room. Most of the patrons had opted for Ricky's pale-face look, though some were in their natural flesh colored states. The women were, by and large, adorned with thick black eyeliner, and Dana and I would have stood out like sore thumbs in our blonde hair. Everyone was sporting Dracula-black wigs.

"See anything suspicious yet?" Dana asked, whispering in my ear. Her voice had a slight lisp to it due to the fangs.

"Define suspicious."

"Good point."

"Let's look for Becca," I said, eyeing a couple in the corner who were giving each other serious hickeys. At least, I hoped they were just hickeys.

I pulled my cell out and dialed Becca's number, on the off chance she might pick up. Or we might hear a tell-tale ring from someone's corset. Unfortunately, I got the voicemail routine again. Leaving us with only the low-tech route to finding our suspect.

We circled our way around the downstairs, passing through groups of cocktail-drinking partygoers (God, I hoped they were cocktails!), snippets of conversation floating past us as we searched their faces for the girl we'd seen with Alexa at the Crush. While she'd been a redhead there, I didn't put it past her to don a wig like Dana and I had. Especially if she was in fugitive mode.

While most of the party-goers were in some sort of affected state of undead make-up, I was surprised to see the majority were middle aged, average looking, every-day people that one might encounter in line at Starbucks. Heck, take away the capes and white foundation and you had any other party in the Hollywood Hills.

All except for one person.

As we rounded the corner into the study, I spied Sebastian chatting with a woman in another long, black wig. He stood near an enormous, seven-foot-tall fireplace, a crackling fire filling its mouth despite the California heat. His long legs were encased in another pair of crisp slacks, his black button down shirt opened at the collar. His spiked hair was messed into an effortless style, and I could see the glint off his fangs in the glow cast by the antique chandelier above his head.

As if he could feel me watching him, his gaze suddenly turned toward mine. His unnaturally blue eyes (which had to be just contacts, right?) held mine for a half-second. Just long enough to make me wonder if my disguise was all that disguising after all. Then he turned his attention back to his companion.

Despite the heat from the fire, I felt a chill run up my spine. I tried to tell myself it was just fear of getting caught and not fear of having my bodily fluids drained, but I grabbed Dana by the arm just the same.

"Let's get out of here," I lisped in Cindy Brady fashion into her ear. "We haven't checked for Becca upstairs yet."

Dana nodded, and we quickly backed out of the room, slipping into the hallway where a large staircase spiraled up to the next floor. The second I was out of Sebastian's presence, I felt a sigh of relief sweep over me. Supernatural or not, that guy had an unnerving effect that made me jealous of Marco sitting in the nice, safe car outside. The sooner we found Becca and got out of there, the better.

At the top of the stairs, the landing gave way to another series of rooms. Fewer people were mingling up here than in the lower part of the house, and Dana and I quickly made our way through the first three rooms with no sign of our MIA redhead, before pausing outside of what looked like a master bedroom.

"Should we go in?" Dana whispered, looking over her shoulder.

"I guess we should. I mean, no stone unturned."

"You wanna go first?"

"Nope."

Dana sighed. "Okay," she said with her hand on the doorknob, "but I swear to God, if I find a coffin in there…"

I elbowed her in the ribs. "You have been spending way too much time with Marco." Though, I'll admit I let out a small sigh of relief when we saw a king sized bed under a paisley-printed quilt stare back at us.

"See. He's just a guy who likes to wear fangs," I said, much more confidently than I felt.

"Uh huh," Dana said, moving toward the closet. "And apparently women's clothes?" She held up a tiny, black dress with a one-shoulder strap.

Which was an exact match for the one Becca had been wearing the night of the murder.

I felt my heart skip a beat, landing somewhere in my throat. "Ohmigod, that's Becca's dress!"

I almost hated to look, but…

I leaned in close, squinting at the dark fabric for any sign of Alexa's blood.

Dana did the same. "I don't see anything on it," she finally concluded.

I nodded. "Me neither. Still, what's it doing in here?"

Dana shook her head. "I don't know. But it's pretty solid evidence that Sebastian knows more than he's telling us."

"Agreed. And it's time we found out what," I decided, taking the dress from Dana and making for the study with the enormous fireplace again.

Only we never quite made it.

We got as far as the bottom of the stairs when a woman in a long, flowing maxi-dress darted from the study, slamming squarely into both Dana and I.

"Uhn," I said, feeling the wind get knocked out of me. Which, honestly, didn't take much. The trip down the stairs had been enough to bring me to half-wind already.

"Hey, watch it. She's pregnant!" Dana shouted at the woman.

She turned around only briefly to acknowledge our presence before continuing her flight.

But it was enough for me to recognize her face and the distinct strands of red hair peeking out from a wig fallen askew in her haste.

Becca.

CHAPTER ELEVEN

———

"Becca, wait!" I called, though her retreating back didn't slow down a bit. If anything, she picked up pace, hauling it through the crowd toward the back of the house at lightening speeds.

"I've got her," Dana said, darting after her, pushing her way through the crowd.

I did my best to waddle after them, but the fact was a) I wasn't nearly the gym devotee that Dana as and b) carrying an extra fifteen pounds around kinda put a damper on my efforts. No way was I going to catch up.

I watched the two black wigs bob toward the back of the house, then out the back doors, where I lost them. I pushed my way through the party-goers, hitting the pair of French doors just in time to see two figures in heels and black dresses sprinting across an expanse of manicured lawn behind the house, before they disappeared into a grove of trees. Crap. The heels on these boots were so not made for tramping across a soggy lawn.

"What's going on out there?" a voice said, suddenly at my ear.

I jumped, letting out a little Chihuahua-style yip and spun around to find myself nose-to-nose with Sebastian.

I took one giant step backward.

"Uh, nothing. Just, um, getting a little fresh air."

He cocked his head to the side, his icy eyes pinning me to the spot. "I thought I saw your friend jogging across my lawn just now."

I bit my lip. "Did you?" I squeaked out.

He nodded slowly. "Yes."

"Well, that's Dana. Any excuse for a little exercise." The second the words left my lips I mentally cringed at the lameness of my lying skills.

Luckily, Sebastian let it go.

Unluckily, he took a step forward, uncomfortably closing the gap between us again.

"You know, I don't remember inviting the two of you to this party," he slowly drawled.

I swallowed loudly, my throat suddenly bone dry. "I'll forgive the oversight."

"Hmmm." He narrowed his eyes at me, assessing.

I swallowed again, cleared my throat, and firmly told myself he was just some guy in contacts and a pair of plastic teeth.

"Exactly what are you doing here?" he asked.

"Looking for Becca," I found myself confessing under his steady gaze.

"And did you find her?"

I nodded. "Dana's with her right now," I said, hoping it was the truth. "And," I added, putting on my bravest face, "we found something that belongs to Becca, too."

He slowly raised one eyebrow. "Did you, now?"

"Yes. Her dress. The one she was wearing the night Alexa died."

"Interesting." If the information unnerved him, he didn't show it, his face as impassive as always.

"Want to know where we found it?" I asked, my confidence edging higher.

"I'm all ears."

"Your bedroom."

His jaw flinched, his eyes narrowing ever so slightly as his shoulders tightened. It was an almost imperceptible physical shift, but his entire demeanor suddenly went from mildly amused to somewhere between menacing and downright dangerous.

"Another place I don't believe you were invited to," he responded, his voice an evenly modulated growl.

I licked my lips. "What was the dress doing there?"

But instead of answering me, he wrapped a hand around my upper arm. "I think it's time for you to go," he said, steering me out the door.

"Did Becca come here after the club?" I persisted. "Did she tell you what happened? Did she tell you Alexa was dead? Did she need your help cleaning up the murder?"

"You ask a lot of questions, Miss Springer," he said, leading me around the side of the building, back toward the circular drive.

"You don't answer very many," I shot back.

"No. I don't."

"And it's Mrs., by the way," I corrected him. I'm married."

"Lucky man," he mumbled, though I wasn't entirely sure whether or not I detected a note of sarcasm.

"Look, we're just trying to find out what happened to Alexa," I said as the rows of cars came back into view. I could vaguely make out Marco's form slouched in the passenger seat of Dana's Mustang. "If you're innocent, then you have nothing to hide," I reasoned.

Sebastian stopped walking abruptly, turning me around to face him. His eyes shone eerily in the moonlight, making me involuntarily lean back.

"We all have something to hide, Mrs. Springer," he said, his voice flat and low.

And with that, he turned and left me standing on the paved drive as he walked back through the mahogany front doors of his Castle of Creepiness.

Despite my disappointment at getting more questions than answers from him, I did a shiver of relief at being out of there, then quickly power-walked over to the car.

"Are you okay?" Marco hissed as soon as I had the doors open. "I saw you talking with the vampire. God, he was leaning so close to you that I was sure he was going to dig right into your neck."

"I'm fine," I answered. Even though a teeny tiny part of me might have shared his fear.

"Good. Here," he said, passing me my tote bag again.

I took it, feeling a distinctly soggy spot at the bottom. "What happened to it?"

"I think your fake baby may have wet itself."

I peeked inside. Sure enough, there was a wet stain in the front of Baby-So-Lifelike's yellow onesie. Fab.

I was just drying off the tubes of lipgloss at the bottom of my tote with a fast-food napkin from the glove box when Dana pulled the door open, sliding into the driver's seat, her breath coming hard.

"Did you catch her?" I asked, hoping at least our entire evening hadn't been a bust.

She shook her head, panting as she tried to catch her breath. "No. She had too much of a lead."

I felt my shoulders sag. "Did you see where she went?"

Dana nodded, sucking in big gulps of air. "Into a car. It was waiting at the bottom of the hill."

"I don't suppose you got the license plate number?" I asked.

Dana grinned, then reached into her purse and pulled out a slip of paper with seven numbers and letters written on it. "Now what kind of Cagney would I be if I didn't?"

* * *

We agreed to meet the next morning to track down a name to go with the license number, and half an hour later Dana dropped me off in front of my house. Surprisingly, there was already a car parked in my driveway. A big, black SUV with a red police siren plunked on the dash. I raised an eyebrow. Could it be that my husband was actually home? Maybe my luck was turning around this evening.

"Honey, I'm ho-ome," I sing-songed as I pushed through the front door.

Ramirez was on the sofa, a stack of papers in hand again. He looked up as soon as I walked in, took in my attire, and blinked hard.

"What is *that*?"

I looked down. "What?"

Ramirez raised an eyebrow at me. "The outfit, doll."

"Oh. This?" I blinked innocently. It's the latest-"

"And don't tell me," he said, cutting me off, "that this is the latest fashion trend."

I shut my mouth with a click. Damn, he knew me so well. "Okay, fine. Dana and I were at a costume party tonight."

The eyebrow didn't lower. "Costume party, huh? What kind of costume party?"

"The kind where you dress up."

"As?"

"Vamphrauhs."

"Did you just mumble on purpose?" he asked, still giving me The Look.

"I did not," I protested. Okay, honestly? I kinda did.

"Uh huh. What kind of party, Springer?"

I blew out a breath. "Fine. You win. We were at a vampire party."

"Jesus," Ramirez mumbled under his breath. "Please don't tell me this has anything to do with your harebrained theory about Alexa's death."

"Okay." I paused, letting silence settle between us.

"Well?" he finally prompted.

"You told me *not* to tell you."

Ramirez clenched his jaw shut, and about ten really dirty words flashed behind his eyes. "Maddie, I love you."

"I love you, too, honey," I said, dripping with sweetness.

"But you drive me insane."

"In a good way?" I asked, ever hopeful.

"In a way that makes we wish I'd married a woman who isn't fascinated by murder."

"I am not fascinated," I protested.

"Just nosey?" he offered.

I swatted him in the arm. "Watch it, buster."

"Look, just this once could you leave the investigation to the authorities?"

"I would love to," I promised him. "But the authorities aren't looking in the right places."

Ramirez looked down at my outfit again. "And you are?"

"Yes! Look, someone went through a lot of trouble to make it look like Alexa was killed by a vampire. Don't you think that's significant?"

"I think the evidence will tell us what's significant."

"Well, did you know that Alexa actually *worked* as a vampire?"

"Yes."

I shut my mouth with a click. "Oh." That was not the answer I'd been anticipating. "You did?"

"Maddie, I'm a homicide detective. You think I wouldn't look into where the victim worked?"

Right. He had a point. "Okay, well, do you know that her friend, the last person to see her alive *and* the girl who also worked with Alexa as a vampire, is now on the run?"

He paused.

"Ha! Gotcha." I couldn't help the triumph in my voice.

Ramirez shook his head, though I could see the faintest hint of smile playing at the corner of his lips. "Okay, Maddie, define 'on the run.'"

"She took off from the club after Alexa died, and her clothes are all packed, and she's been missing ever since."

"So she hasn't been in to work at her vampire job?"

"Well, yes, she was tonight, but then she took off. *Running.*"

The corners of his mouth quirked upward. "I see."

"You're humoring me, aren't you?" I asked, narrowing my eyes at him.

He held up his thumb and index finger. "Just a little."

"You know, if I wasn't aware that our baby already has ears, I'd have a few choice words for you right now, pal."

"Okay, fine," he said, holding up his hands in a mock surrender gesture. "I'll admit the friend might be worth talking to. I promise I'll look into it, okay?"

"Thank you," I said, triumph nudging into my voice again.

"But don't think this means I'm okay with you running around town with a bunch of crazy *Moonlight* wannabes," he quickly added.

"Fair enough," I agreed. Hey, he said he wasn't okay with it, not that I had to stop. If he wanted to get bent out of shape over it, that was his prerogative.

"Where did you get that crazy outfit anyway?" he asked, that hint of a smile playing at his lips again as he eyed the black stockings peeking out of my Victorian ankle boots.

"The set of *Moonlight II.*"

That hint broke into the real deal. "I rest my case."

"Come on," I said, punching him in the arm again. "Don't you think the whole vampire thing is just a little bit sexy?"

Ramirez looked down at my fishnets again and grinned. "Maybe. Just a little bit."

"You know…" I said, taking a step closer. "I don't have to give the costume back until tomorrow…."

Ramirez paused a moment, looked down at my dress again, going from the low neckline, to the healthy dose of cleavage the empire cut popped upward, to the touchably soft velvet trialing down my torso...

Then his eyes hit The Bump and immediately turned from dark chocolate to a flat brown.

"You know, I'm just not really in the mood tonight, Maddie."

I blinked. Trying to process the words that had just come out of his mouth. My husband, the testosterone machine, the walking sex drive, was not in the mood. Not in the mood! What the hell was that supposed to mean?!

"What is that supposed to mean?" I blurted out before I could pause to decide if I really wanted to hear the answer to that question.

Ramirez cleared his throat and focused really hard on a non-existent piece of lint on his sleeve. "It just means that I still have a lot of paperwork to do tonight."

"A lot of work."

"And I'm kind of tired."

"Kind of tired."

"And I have a bit of a headache."

"A bit of a headache," I repeated doing a fabulous imitation of a parrot as my mind went nuts trying to read between his lines.

"Look, I'm gonna go call in this info about Alexa's missing friend," he said, looking everywhere but at me and my fishnets now.

"Uh huh. Sure. Great." I watched his retreating back duck into the other room and close the door, not sure if I wanted to scream at him, cry, or just plain give up.

CHAPTER TWELVE

———

"Ramirez thinks I'm fat."

Dana gasped and put a hand over her mouth. "He did *not* say that!"

I shrugged. "He didn't say it, but he won't sleep with me," I told her over what was fast becoming our morning chamomile ritual. "And I'm sure it's because I'm fat."

"You are not fat," Dana said. "You're pregnant."

"Dana, you are a great friend. But there is not a baby in my ass, and my ass has grown to twice its size. That is a fat ass."

Dana peeked behind me. She bit her lip. "It's just to balance out the front. If your butt didn't grow, you might fall right over forward."

"Fab. So I'm exponentially expanding all over?"

"I've heard that breastfeeding makes the pounds melt right off," Dana reassured me.

"So I might be able to lose the ass, but I'm trading it in for saggy breasts?"

"Don't worry," Dana said, waving me off. "There's always plastic surgery for that. Oh, have you heard of the mommy makeover?"

I hated to ask… "What's the mommy makeover?"

"Ohmigod, it's great. They do your breast, tummy, and saddlebags all at the same time."

"Saddlebags?" My eyes flew to my thighs. "I don't have saddle bags, too, do I?"

Dana blinked at me. "No. Of course not," she said, her eyes wide and innocent.

"Oh, God, that's your lying face. I do have saddlebags!"

"I think we need more tea," Dana said, getting up to refill my mug.

I thunked my head down on the kitchen table, doing deep, Lamaze breaths, willing myself to come to terms with my whale-like status. It was just temporary, right? With enough hours on the Stairmaster after the baby came, I'm sure I could shrink my ass back to normal size. Some pec-working push-ups, and my boobs would perk right back up. A couple of sea-weed wraps, and I'm sure my thighs would smooth out. And if all that failed, I made a plan to start a mommy make-over fund as soon as my next paycheck arrived.

"You okay?" Dana said, setting my mug in front of me. "'Cause you kinda sound like you're hyperventilating."

I paused mid-deep breath. "I'm fine," I lied. "Look, let's just drop the whole subject and go look up that license plate number, okay?"

"Right," Dana agreed. "So, where's Ramirez's computer?"

"Spare room," I directed, grabbing my mug and leading the way to our guest bedroom slash storage room slash Ramirez's office slash the baby's room.

"Whoa," Dana said stepping through the doorway. "What happened in here?"

I watched her wide eyes take in the room. A stack of Tupperware boxes filled with holiday decorations took up one end and a wardrobe rack filled with overflow from my closet the other. A crib sat at the far side under the window, though it was filled to the top with baby items, still in their packages. Humidifiers, wipes warmers, bottle sanitizers, and about a million other things that I wasn't sure what they did but my mom had insisted that her grandbaby needed. There was a twin bed somewhere under a pile of baby clothes, and in the far corner was a desk where a laptop hunkered down amidst piles of papers.

I guess all the slashes in our room's use had kinda filled it to max.

"It's a little messy, I know," I admitted.

"Messy? Dude, I'm about to dial *Hoarders* on you."

"I'm going to clear it out before the baby comes."

She looked down at me. Back up at the mess. "You sure you have enough time?"

"Let's just run the plate," I said, stepping over a baby excer-saucer and a package of diapers to get to the laptop.

I jiggled the mouse to life, pulling up Ramirez's desktop. In the top corner was an icon labeled CADMV. I clicked it, and the Department of Motor Vehicles program immediately popped up, a window appearing that prompted me for a password.

"You know the password?" Dana asked, watching the screen over my shoulder.

I shook my head. "Not exactly." I tried his date of birth, then hit enter.

The screen blinked at me, then displayed a line of text stating I had entered an incorrect password, prompting me to try again.

So, I did. I entered my date of birth. Our wedding date. Our address, phone number, and any other combo of numbers I could think of, before turning to words he might use. I started with "cop", moved on to "homicide" and even "lapddude", before finally drawing a blank.

"I'm stumped," I confessed.

"Here, let me try," Dana said, dragging the keyboard her direction. After a couple of combos of numbers and letters, she finally smiled, a light bulb going off behind her eyes. "Duh!" she said, her fingers flying. I saw her type in the word "Maddie", and hit enter.

And the screen switched to the database homepage.

I grinned sheepishly, feeling a flutter of warm fuzzies in my stomach. Okay, so maybe our sex life wasn't making like rabbits lately, but my husband was thinking of me even when he was running bad guys' license plates. In a weird way, that was kind of romantic.

"We're in," Dana announced, pulling the slip of paper from last night out of her pocket. She quickly typed in the digits she'd written down, hit enter, and we waited a beat before the program spit back a name associated with the vehicle: Lawrence Goldstein. I grabbed a Babies-R-Us receipt from the crib and wrote down the address displayed beneath his name on the back. It was in downtown L.A., and, half an hour later, we were standing in front of it, looking up at a high-rise that gleamed against the bright morning sunshine.

We entered the lobby, which was white marble floors, sleek modern chairs, and a bustle of people filtering past a large, cherry reception desk manned by four women in black headsets.

Dana and I approached, asking the first one where we could find Lawrence Goldstein's offices. She indicated the elevators, saying he was on the seventh floor.

We thanked her, rode the elevator, and got out at the law offices of Goldstein and Associates, Attorneys at Law, or so the gold plaque above a second cherry reception desk told us. Like the first one, she was wearing another black headset. "May I help you?" she asked as we approached.

"Yes, we'd like to see Mr. Goldstein, please," I told her.

She nodded, glancing briefly down at a computer screen. "Do you have an appointment?"

"Uh, no. I'm sorry, we don't," I confessed.

"And what is this matter regarding?" she asked.

"It's kind of confidential," Dana jumped in.

The receptionist raised an eyebrow, but must have seen enough confidentially minded people filter into her offices that she didn't ask. Instead, she indicated a pair of chairs. "Have a seat, and I'll see if he can fit you in."

We did, though I'd scarcely gotten through the first article in the *People* magazine on the coffee table before she told us to go down the hallway to the right and enter the last pair of doors.

We did, finding ourselves in reception number three.

"May I help you?" asked a younger, blonder version of the first two women in black headsets.

"We're here to see Mr. Goldstein," I repeated.

She nodded. "Through the first door on the left," she said, indicating another doorway.

I gingerly pushed through, wondering just how many gatekeepers Mr. Goldstein had. Thankfully, instead of another headset, behind the low cherry desk in this room sat an older man that I hoped was Goldstein.

He was in his fifties, if I had to guess, his salt and pepper hair turned mostly to salt at this point. He was solidly built, though his cheeks had started to go slack around the jowls, giving his face a bulldog look. Adding to the canine image, his eyes were small, set far apart in his face, and, at the moment, sharply intent on Dana and me.

"I'm Larry Goldstein," he said, rising from behind his desk to shake our hands.

"Maddie Springer," I offered. "And this is my friend, Dana Dashel."

"Very nice to meet you," he said, sitting again. "How may I help you ladies?"

"We wanted to ask you a few questions," I started.

He raised one bushy eyebrow. "Such as?"

"How well do you know Becca Diamond?" Dana blurted out.

He frowned, his forehead wrinkling. "Who?"

"Don't play coy with us," Dana said, taking a menacing step forward. Well, as menacing as a blonde in a mini skirt and three inch heels can be. "We saw you pick her up in your car last night."

The frown between his bushy eyebrows intensified. "You mean Willow?"

I cocked my head to the side. "I mean the redhead in the black dress and dark wig who jumped into your car outside Sebastian's place."

"Right," he agreed, the confusion lifting. "Willow Morte."

"A stage name?" I asked.

He shrugged. "I don't know. All I know is she said her name was Willow."

"Okay, fine. So how well do you know Willow?"

"Why do you want to know about her?"

"We have some… issues to discuss with her. And we're having a hard time reaching her."

He sucked in his cheeks, nodding. But whether he bought the line or not, he seemed curious enough to continue the conversation.

"I knew her casually," he said. "I've seen her at a few parties."

"Sebastian's vampire parties? So, you're a frequent guest?"

His cheeks tinged red above his starchy collar. "Well, I wouldn't say frequent, but I do attend from time to time."

"And that's where you met Willow?"

He nodded. "But I wouldn't say I know her well."

"Well enough to take her home last night," Dana pointed out.

He paused, looking from Dana to me. "What exactly is this about?"

"Alexa Weston," Dana answered. "Did you know her, too?"

Goldstein gave Dana a blank look. Either he had no idea who she was talking about, or it was a fabulous poker face.

"You may have known her by a stage name, too," I added. "She was Willow's friend. Long black hair, pale skin, super skinny."

Goldstein slowly nodded. "I think I know the girl. What about her?"

I bit my lip. Apparently he hadn't heard. "Alexa was murdered three nights ago."

I could see Goldstein would be a champion in the courtroom. His face was a total blank, any emotion he may have felt at the passing of the "immortal" Alexa was completely hidden. For a second, I wondered if he'd even heard me.

Finally, he spoke again. "I'm very sorry to hear that," he said, his voice a flat monotone.

"When was the last time you saw Alexa?" I asked, trying to pull something out of him.

He paused, choosing his words carefully. "Last week. Sebastian had a party, and I attended."

"And both Alexa and Becca were in attendance, too?"

He nodded. "Yes."

"Where did you take Becca last night?" Dana asked.

I watched Goldstein mentally try on several different answers before he finally settled on, "Why do you want to know?"

"Becca was the last person seen with Alexa before she died."

"And we think she knows something about Alexa's death," Dana added.

Goldstein shook his head. "No. You must be mistaken. Becca is not that kind of girl."

"So you *do* know her well," I said.

He paused, looking from Dana to me, trying to assess just how much he should tell us. Finally he nodded. "Fine. Yes. I knew Becca well enough to know she would never kill someone. She was a sweet girl."

I narrowed my eyes at him. "Sweet" was not exactly the kind of word I'd expect anyone to use when describing the girls I'd met at Crush. Which made me wonder...

"Were you sleeping with her?"

Goldstein's cheeks immediately went screaming red. "I'm a married man," he said holding up his left hand clad in a thick, gold band on the ring finger.

"That doesn't answer my question."

"I'll have you know that I love my wife very much."

I nodded. "But you were sleeping with Becca?"

"This is preposterous. I don't have to answer these kinds of questions," he said, shaking his head so that his bulldog jowls wiggled like Jell-o.

Honestly? His lack of denial already kind of had. "Okay, let's go back to Alexa," I said, backing away from the touchy subject. "When did you say the last time you saw her was?"

For once, he seemed glad to answer a question, gratefully jumping on the subject change.

"Last week. Alexa came up to me at the party saying she needed some legal advice."

"About what?" I asked.

He shook his head. "I never found out. I told her to drop by my office, but she said that was too risky. She said she'd meet me at the party last night. I was there, but she never showed up."

"But Becca did," I broke in.

He nodded. "She came running up to me and said she needed to leave right away."

"Why? What was she running from?" I asked, even though if I had to guess a murder rap would be at the top of my list.

Goldstein shrugged. "She didn't say. But she was shaken up enough that I agreed to drive her home."

"So, you went back to her place?" Dana asked.

Goldstein paused again, licking his lips. I could tell he wasn't the kind of person who said a single thing without first deliberating. A great courtroom skill, but it made for an annoying interview process.

"Not exactly," he finally said.

"What do you mean?" I pressed.

"Well, she was antsy. Kept looking out the back window, like she thought someone was following her."

"Who?"

"She didn't say."

"So, what happened?"

"As soon as we turned onto Victory, she said she'd walk the rest of the way and got out of the car."

"Victory?" I asked, hearing the confusion in my own voice. That was a good ten miles from Becca's place off Sunset. "Did you see where she went?"

Goldstein slowly shook his head. "She headed east, toward Lankershim. I figured she lived nearby."

Only we knew for a fact that she didn't.

Meaning, once again, Becca was in the wind.

CHAPTER THIRTEEN

———

I tried dialing Becca's number again, but there was, predictably, no answer. Just for kicks, Dana and I drove by her building again, but there was no sign of her. And after Dana climbed the four flights of stairs (thankfully she let me hang in the lobby as backup), there was no sign that Becca had been back to her trashed place, either.

After circling the block a couple of times for any sign of a redhead in a black wig, Dana dropped me off back at home. Where I was surprised to find not only Ramirez's black SUV in the drive (before 5 PM even!), but also a shiny, silver mini-van with an "I heart my hairdresser" sticker on the bumper.

Uh oh. Mom was here.

I cautiously walked through the door, only to find Ramirez being held captive in the kitchen by my mom and her best friend, Mrs. Rosenblatt. He was holding a hot water bottle in one hand and a tennis ball in the other. Mom had Baby-So-Lifelike in her arms, and Mrs. Rosenblatt was holding a stopwatch.

"Do I even want to know?" I asked, already knowing the answer to that question.

"Madison Louise Springer," my mother said, immediately turning on me. "Do you know where I found my grandbaby this afternoon?"

I blinked. "Uh… hi. Nice to see you, too."

"He was on the floor. Face down. Under a pile of shoes!" She held Baby-So-Lifelike to her chest. "The poor dear could have suffocated."

"He's plastic."

"He's a practice baby, and so far you are indicating that you need a whole lot more practice before you can be trusted with a real baby. Maddie, you left him alone in the house all day. You can't leave a baby alone! This is the ficus all over again."

Oh, brother.

I looked to Ramirez for help, but found him edging himself slowly out of the room.

"And where do you think you're going?" Mom asked, turning on him.

Ramirez froze like a deer in the headlights of a GMC barreling down the 15. "Uh… I thought we were done?"

"Done with what?" I asked, my gaze pinging between the tennis ball and Mrs. Rosenblatt's stopwatch.

"Timing your exit strategy to the hospital," Mrs. R explained.

Mrs. Rosenblatt was a three-hundred pound, five-time divorcee who talked to the dead. She did a weekly astrology column for a local tabloid and ran a psychic reading booth down on the Venice boardwalk on the weekends. She spent weekdays alternating between a booth at Ira's Deli on Highland and my mom's living room, sipping coffee and gossiping about the neighbors. Her wardrobe consisted of a never-ending supply of brightly colored muumuus and Crocks. Today's offering was a hot pink tent with neon yellow daisies printed all over it. Which perfectly matched the neon yellow eye shadow extending clear to her painted-on eyebrows. To say Mrs. Rosenblatt was a bit eccentric was like saying Lindsey Lohan was a bit of an alcoholic. However this was Hollywood, so honestly, she didn't stick out all that much.

"So far," she informed me, looking down at the stopwatch, "your husband is at just under twenty minutes.

Though we took off ten minutes because he had to go looking for the tennis ball in the garage."

"I'm confused. Tennis ball?"

"In case you have back labor," Mom said. "It's very common in our family."

"We're aiming for fifteen minutes flat to get you out of here," Mrs. R said, resetting the stopwatch. "So the big guy here's gotta pick up the pace."

"And even fifteen isn't that much time when you take into consideration travel time," Mom added. She paused. "You do have your travel route to the hospital planned out, right?"

I blinked. "Uh…"

"Good lord, Maddie! You don't know how to get to the hospital?" My mom's face went white. "My first grandson is going to be born in traffic on the 405. I just know it."

"Mom, *she*'s not due for another four months. We have time," I argued.

"Babies come early, you know," Mom said, wagging a manicured fingernail at me.

"Like Kyle Morganthwait," Mrs. Rosenblatt agreed, nodding sagely.

"Who?" I asked.

"My third husband's cousin's daughter's kid," Mrs. R explained. "Little Kyle was born three months early. Only weighed a single pound."

I looked down at my belly. Could it really be that The Bump only weighed a pound? Good lord, where had the other fifteen I'd gained gone?

"Don't panic," Mom said, putting up a hand. "I'll find a route to the hospital."

"You're the only one panicking, Mom," I pointed out. "And I really think Ramirez and I are capable of finding the hospital."

But she completely ignored me, making for the spare room and Ramirez's laptop.

I followed a reluctant step behind, watching her navigate around the diapers, jiggle the mouse to life and pull up Google Maps.

"Okay, so if you take the 405 to Santa Monica to Beverly, it should only take you twenty minutes."

"If there's no traffic," Mrs. Rosenblatt interjected, coming into the room behind us. "If it's past 3 PM, you're gonna want to take surface streets all the way."

"But not Santa Monica," Mom added. "In that case, you'll want to take the canyon, coming out on Sunset and cutting through town."

"Unless you get car sick," Mrs. R amended. "Then you should go the 101 route, taking Melrose to La Cienega. And in that case, you'd better have your tennis balls ready to go, because that could be a full forty minute ride."

"She can put them in her overnight bag, right Maddie?" Mom said.

I blinked.

"Oh, God, Maddie, please tell me you have an overnight bag ready to go?"

I shook my head. "Honestly, I'm not planning to stay overnight."

"What?" Mom froze at the keyboard.

"The hospital only requires a twelve hour stay," I explained. "If we go in the morning, we'll be home by dinner."

"And what if the baby comes in the middle of the night?" Mom asked.

"Well, I'm sure that could happen, but-"

"Or what if you end up needing a C-section," Mrs. Rosenblatt added.

I cringed involuntarily at the idea of scalpels anywhere in the vicinity of my skin. "I'm sure we won't need to-"

"Or what," Mom jumped in again, "if you have a long labor?"

"That's right," Mrs. Rosenblatt agreed. "My second husband's first wife was in labor with their son, Tommy, for thirty-six hours."

"Thirty-*six*?" I squeaked out. I suddenly felt faint.

"Don't panic," my Mom repeated. "I'll pack you a bag. I'll be sure to put lots of cozy nightgowns in it.

The last time I wore a "nightgown" I was five. But I didn't argue, still trying to wrap my brain around the idea of being in labor for a full three days. That must be a mistake. That can't be normal. I mean, *What to Expect When You're Expecting* said nothing about thirty-six hours. Surely *What to Expect When You're Expecting* would have told me if I should expect thirty-six hours. It mentioned three stages of labor, but I was pretty sure I could knock each one out in an hour. Two tops, if I was determined.

"…and then… Maddie are you listening?"

I realized I wasn't. I'd been too busy not panicking. "Sorry, what?"

"I was saying that when they put in the epidural-"

But I put up a hand to stop her. "Stop right there. I'm not planning to have an epidural."

Mom and Mrs. Rosenblatt turned to me as one, looks of horror on their faces like I'd just said I was going to roller skate down the Venice boardwalk without pants.

"What do you mean no epidural?" Mom asked.

"I want to have a natural birth."

"Good lord, why?" Mrs. Rosenblatt asked.

"Because the fewer the drugs, the safer it is for the baby. Besides, my Lamaze teacher says that we can use proper breathing techniques, and with each contraction my endorphins will kick in to provide a natural pain reliever."

Mom stared at me. She blinked. Then she burst into laughter. "Oh honey, that's the funniest thing I've ever heard in my life."

Okay, this conversation was going downhill fast. "Look, I'm fine. Ramirez and I have a natural birth plan worked out with our Lamaze coach. We can find the hospital. We'll be great. Thanks so much for all your help," I said, ushering her ever so gently out of the room and toward the front door.

"My fifth husband, Buck, was all into that natural stuff, too," Mrs. R said, nodding. "He died at age forty. Had a wheat grass blockage in his colon."

"Greatseeingyou, thanksforstoppingby, seeyousoon," I said all in one breath as I shut the door behind them.

I let out a long sigh, then turned around to see Ramirez, still standing in the kitchen, staring after them, a shell-shocked look on his face. "I don't know what I'm supposed to do with this tennis ball."

If I didn't know better, I'd say Bad Cop was actually scared.

* * *

While Ramirez reheated a tamale casserole, courtesy of his mother again (I don't know why people are so down on mother-in-laws. I was kinda in love with mine lately.), I settled in at the laptop and a) tried not to think about labor, back or otherwise, b) tried not to think about where my husband was planning to sleep tonight, and c) tried to focus in on just who might have wanted Alexa dead.

I started by googling the term "vampires".

Okay, let's face it, Ramirez was right on one account – all I knew about vampires I learned from *Moonlight*. Which maybe wasn't the most definitive source out there. And considering everything in this case seemed to point back to them, I figured I'd better educate myself about my subject.

An hour and six tamales later (Hey, if The Bump only weighed a pound, I had to fatten her up.), I had found out three things:

1. There is a proportionally large number of the online population that think they are actual bloodsuckers

2. Everyone on Facebook couldn't wait for the *Moonlight* sequel and

3. It's a lot harder than Hollywood would have you believe to drain the blood from a person.

This last fact was courtesy of a woman who called herself the Vamp Doc, and had a blog article explaining just what it took to drain a body of blood.

Apparently the rate at which someone would naturally bleed out depends on which artery is punctured. An average person has five to six liters of blood. The heart circulates this entire amount every minute. So, depending on the size and location of a puncture wound, it's possible to drain a person's entire blood supply in just over a minute.

In theory. But, as Vamp Doc went on to say, those are under ideal (or non-ideal, depending on your point of view) conditions. In a typical "vampire" biting, the puncture wounds would be small enough that the heart wouldn't pump out at maximum volume. However, she estimated that it would only take a total of two to three minutes before an individual would lose two-and-a-half to three liters of blood, a sufficient amount to cause loss of consciousness and death.

Which was plenty of time for our killer to off Alexa in the bathroom stall. Assuming that the killer punctured her neck and drained her of blood, it would have taken no more than five minutes tops, and the killer would have been on her way.

The only snag would have been I doubted Alexa would let someone drain her of blood without a struggle.

Sure she was into the scene, but at some point she must have realized that they weren't playing. So how come there was no sign of a struggle? No blood anywhere at the scene?

"What's that?" Ramirez asked, coming up behind me, a plate of cookies in hand. Chocolate chip, if my nose didn't deceive me.

I quickly shut the laptop screen.

"What?" I asked innocently.

He shot me a look. "Did I just see fangs on that website?"

"I don't know. Did you?"

"Luuucy," he said, doing his best Ricky Ricardo.

I rolled my eyes. "Fine, yes. I'm researching vampires. Happy?"

"You know what would make me happy?" Ramirez asked, setting the plate down on top of a diaper genie box. "A wife who sits at home and knits. Or bakes. Or even does crossword puzzles."

"Boring," I decreed, grabbing a cookie. "What fun would that be?"

He grinned, showing off the dimple in his left cheek. "You're right. No fun at all," he teased.

I grinned back.

But then the weirdest thing happened. A film of awkward settled in the room between us. See, normally, this is where he'd make some sexual comment, do those dark, chocolate eyes at me, I'd melt into a puddle, and then he'd scoop me into his arms and we'd hit the bedroom.

Only his eyes weren't dark chocolate right now. They were just a slightly amused brown. And he wasn't making sexual comments. In fact, his eyes were straying to the pile of paperwork beside the laptop more than they were to me. And I was way too big to be scooped by anyone.

It was almost as if I could feel the chemistry between us dying a slow, painful death as we sat there grinning stupidly at each other.

Okay, I had two choices here. I could either grow a pair and ask my husband why he didn't want to sleep with me… resulting in most likely being rejected for the second night in a row and possibly hearing the dreaded truth that my gargantu-butt no longer turned him on. Or, I could instead take the plate of cookies, get into my Snuggie, and go watch *Moonlight* for the eighth time with my good pal, Denial.

The cookies were chocolate chip. The decision was a no brainer.

I did a yawn that was bordering on uber-fake, stretching my arms above my head. "Well, I'm super tired so I'm gonna go retire early," I told Ramirez.

"Sure. Good idea," he said, his hands already reaching for the papers beside the desk, his eyes not meeting mine as if he'd heard the chemistry die, too. "'Night, Maddie."

I grabbed the plate, shoved another cookie in my mouth as I mumbled, "'Night," and made my way into bed.

Alone.

Again.

CHAPTER FOURTEEN

———

I was chasing her. Running through the streets of downtown L.A. It was dark, the streetlights casting only the faintest glow of light as I watched her red hair disappear around a corner. Amazingly, the street was deserted, something that never actually happened in L.A. It was just her and me. I could hear her breath coming hard, was sure I was catching up to her.

"Becca!" I called out. But she didn't stop, didn't slow down. Just kept running.

I continued following her, but the faster I needed to go, the slower it seemed my feet would move. It was like the sidewalk was suddenly made of molasses, every step a struggle. And I could see her getting away, pulling farther and farther ahead of me until all I could see was the faintest outline of her shape.

"Becca!" I called out to her again.

But a deep voice behind me responded, "Forget her."

I stopped running and spun around to find myself face to face with Sebastian. His icy blue eyes were bearing down on me, his hair shining like dangerous spikes in the glow of the lamps above us.

"She's gone," he told me. "But I need to replace her."

He took a step forward. "I want you to replace her."

I opened my mouth to protest, to scream, but no sound came out. Instead, I felt myself gasping for air as

Sebastian's eyes turned wild, his lips parting, and his fangs gleaming under the streetlamps as he reached for my neck…

The sound of the William Tell Overture screamed from my nightstand, jerking me awake. I took three deep breaths, pulling myself out of my dream and back into reality as I glared at the alarm clock numbers glowing red next to me. 7:30 AM. Reluctantly I fumbled in my sleep-haze until my fingers connected with my cell, and I managed to stab the on button.

"Hello?" I croaked out.

"He didn't come home last night," Dana whimpered on the other end.

"Who?"

"Ricky! Maddie, he didn't come home last night. He's out with Ava. That's it, I've lost him to a *Playboy* vamp-bunny!"

I blinked, rubbing sleep from my eyes. "You're sure he's out with Ava?"

"Where else could he be?"

"Maybe he was shooting last night?"

I heard Dana nodding on the other end. "Uh huh. He was. But the shoot was over at six, and it's now seven-thirty, and he isn't home."

I did a mental eye roll. "An hour and a half? Honey that's not a 'he didn't come home last night,' that's a 'he's stuck in traffic on the 101.'"

"This is what she's doing to me," Dana said, her voice rising into the hysterics zone. "Thanks to that full frontal twit I can't eat, I can't sleep, all I think about is Ricky signing another contract to let her sink her fangs into my boyfriend's neck."

"I'm sure Ricky's on his way. Did you try calling him?"

"His cell is off." Dana paused. "Oh God. His cell is off. That's a bad sign, isn't it? That's a sign he doesn't want me to know where he is. He's sleeping with her, isn't he? He's sleeping with her right now with his phone off!"

"Deep breaths. In, out," I instructed.

I heard her comply on the other end, sucking in a gulp of air. "Maddie, you have to come down to the set with me and find him."

"Now?" I asked, glancing at my alarm clock again. 7:32. Still way too early for human contact.

"Please, Maddie. I'm going insane here. I need moral support. I need backup. If I find him naked in her trailer, there's no telling what I might do."

She had a good point. "Give me twenty minutes."

"I love you. I'll be there in ten," Dana promised, then hung up.

I resisted the urge to fall back into my pillows again, instead dragging my tired self into the shower and through the rituals of hair, make-up, tooth brushing. I then crammed myself into a pair of yoga pants (that were only a little tight in the butt), a forgivingly empire waisted baby-doll sundress (that was long enough to cover said butt), and a pair of woven wedges. I was just shoving Baby-So-Lifelike into my bag (this time wrapped in a plastic diaper from one of the many boxes stored in our spare room) when Dana showed up, grabbed me by the arm, and dragged me out to her car.

To say the ride to Sunset Studios was tense was a gross understatement. Dana treated yellow lights like challenges, stop signs like suggestions, and her gas pedal as if it were an icky spider that needed stomped to death, the harder the better. By the time we finally parked in the lot next to the line of golf carts, my knuckles were whiter than a *Moonlight* cast member and were permanently embedded in her dash.

"That's it, next time, I'm driving," I warned her as she grabbed me by the arm and steered me to a golf cart.

Five minutes later we were pulling into the Brooklyn street where the *Moonlight* set was camped out again today. Dana narrowly missed hitting a wardrobe rack as she pulled up next to Ricky's trailer and catapulted herself to his front door, banging on it with both fists.

A moment later, Ricky's head popped out of the door. "Dude, what's going on?" He looked down and saw Dana. "Babe? What are you doing here?"

"What am *I* doing here? What am *I* doing here?! What are *you* doing here?!"

He blinked. "Filming?"

But she pushed past him, storming into the trailer. "Where is she? Where is that pale-faced slut?"

"What is she talking about?" Ricky asked me as I entered a step behind her.

Only I didn't get to answer as Dana turned on him.

"You didn't come home last night," she said, pointing a finger in his face.

Ricky took a step back. "We ran late with filming."

"And you didn't call me?" Dana asked,

Ricky shrugged. "Sorry. I forgot."

"And your phone is off."

"Like I said, we were filming. I didn't want it to go off in the middle of a scene."

"You're not filming now."

Ricky's eyebrows furrowed down. "Babe, what's the big deal?"

"The big deal? The big deal is," Dana said, puffing up her chest like a blowfish trying to scare off a shark, "that I was not able to get hold of my boyfriend who didn't come home last night!"

Ricky blinked at her. "I never come home at night. I've been doing night shoots for the last three weeks."

"But you didn't come home at six either!"

Ricky looked from Dana to me. "Is this for real?" he asked.

Dana threw her hands up. "Ugh, men!"

Ricky opened his mouth to say more, but a PA stuck his head in the door to the trailer. "Ricky?" he asked. "You're needed in make-up."

"Be right there," he promised. Then he turned to Dana. "Look, we'll talk later, 'k? I gotta go." Then he wisely didn't wait for an answer before hightailing it out of the trailer.

Dana sat down on the sofa with a huff that ruffled her blonde bangs. "I swear if he signs that contract, it just might drive me insane."

As much as I would be sad to see the *Moonlight* saga's big screen run end, I had to agree. She was a woman on the edge.

"I'm sure they're close to wrapping, right?" I asked.

Dana nodded. "Yep. Just the sex scene and two more biting scenes and they're done. Thank God!"

I bit my lip, remembering the last biting scene, the one I'd watched with Dana on my sofa. "You know, there's one thing that's been bothering me about Alexa's death: why didn't she struggle?"

Dana frowned. "What do you mean?"

"Well, if it were a blow to the head or a gunshot I'd get how someone could sneak up on her. But dragging her into a bathroom stall, biting her neck and waiting for the blood to drain? That would take some time. Why didn't Alexa fight back?"

"Good point. Maybe she was drugged first?" Dana said.

I nodded. "It's possible. But then, how would Becca get her into the restroom? Alexa was skinny, but so was Becca. I doubt she would have been able to drag her in without attracting attention."

"So, she would have needed help. Someone bigger and stronger," Dana said, following my train of thought.

"Right. But who?" I asked.

But before Dana could answer, a voice piped up from the trailer door. "What about the boyfriend?"

Both of our heads snapped up to find Ava standing in the doorway, wearing a slinky red dress and popping a wad of bubble gum (watermelon if I wasn't mistaken) between ruby red lips that said she'd already done her stint in make-up that morning.

Dana narrowed her eyes. "What do you want?" she asked.

Ava shrugged her shoulders, all wide-eyed innocence. "Nothing. I was just walking by and heard you guys talking about the murder. Ricky told me all about it."

"I'll bet he did," Dana said under her breath.

"Anyway, I was just saying, if you're looking for who killed her, what about the boyfriend?"

I shook my head. "I don't think she was seeing anyone."

"Uh, yeah," Ava argued. "She totally was."

I paused. "Wait – you knew Alexa?"

Ava nodded. "Sure. We did a toothpaste commercial together a couple years ago. I mean, that was back when I was just starting out, so we're not like, close-close anymore or anything, but we're Facebook friends."

Mental forehead smack.

"And she told you she had a boyfriend?"

Ava shrugged. "Well her status has been 'in a relationship' for the past six months."

I suddenly felt like an amateur. Every *CSI* junkie knew that the boyfriend was the first place to look for your killer. But with all the vampire stuff, I'd been so distracted that I'd never even thought to find out if she'd been seeing someone. "Do you happen to know the boyfriend's name?" I asked, mentally crossing my fingers.

Ava scrunched up her nose, her eyes going to the ceiling as if looking for the answer there. "Um, Devin or Darin or something. Not sure. But I know he works at this new club on Sunset."

And I knew him, too, I realized. Darwin. The bartender at Crush the night Alexa died.

CHAPTER FIFTEEN

""Wait," Dana said holding up a hand. "Are you telling me that Alexa's boyfriend was at the club the night that she died?"

Ava gave her a blank look. "I dunno. All I know is the boyfriend is always the first suspect, right?"

Sadly, the ditz had a point. They were. And considering that "opportunity" had just cropped up for the bartender, we definitely needed to investigate both means and motive.

* * *

Half an hour later (which would have been only twenty minutes if I hadn't had to stop to pee at a gas station on La Brea along the way) we were back at Crush. Once inside, we made a bee-line for the bar, where Darwin was busy slicing limes. He glanced up as we entered, and I could have sworn I saw irritation flit cross his features before his "boss's girlfriend" face slipped on.

"What can I do for you ladies today?" he asked, a fake smile showing off a set of unnaturally white teeth.

"You can tell us the truth," Dana said, going all no-nonsense on him.

Darwin paused, raised an eyebrow her way. "The truth? I'm not sure what you're getting at."

"About your relationship with Alexa," I prompted. "You didn't tell us you were dating the dead girl."

His "on" face slipped again, eyes pinging from Dana and back to me again before answering with, "I didn't lie. You didn't ask, I didn't tell."

"A lie of omission," Dana pointed out.

He shrugged. "Not really. As of that night, we were no longer dating. So there wasn't any relationship to talk about."

"Wait, you two broke up the night she died?" I asked, narrowing my eyes at him. Motive-ville here we come!

He nodded. "That's right. So what?"

"So... who broke up with whom?"

He shifted, no longer slicing citrus but, I noticed, still holding the knife in a tight clutch in his right hand. "If you want to know, I broke up with her."

"Why?" I asked.

"Because I was tired of seeing her with other guys," he said, his eyes flashing in away that told me he meant it.

"What other guys?"

"Those vampire freaks."

"That she met at the parties she worked?" I prodded.

"That's right. I mean, who gets paid to hang out with old dudes? Hookers, that's who."

"So Alexa *was* sleeping with the men from the parties."

Darwin paused. "I don't know for sure. I mean, she said she wasn't, but who knows what goes on up there, you know? Bunch of weirdos."

"So, I take it you weren't into the vampire scene?" I asked.

"Hell, no. What do I look like some kind of freak?"

I glanced at his pierced eyebrow, eyelid, nose, and lower lip. Probably best not to answer that question.

"Alexa knew you didn't like her doing the parties?" Dana jumped in.

Darwin nodded again. "Yeah. We fought about it all the time. In fact, last week she promised she was leaving the scene."

My spidey senses started tingling. "Did she say why?"

"Said she didn't need the money anymore. Said she was getting a big payday and would quit the vampire gig."

"But if she said she was going to quit, why did you break up with her over it the night she died?"

His face screwed up into a snarl. "Because she lied."

I raised an eyebrow. "How so?"

"I saw her that night with one of those freaks. Clearly she'd just been playin' me about quitting. So, I told her it was over."

"And how did she take that?" Dana asked.

He shrugged. "What did I care? I'd wasted enough time on her."

His compassion for the dead girl was overwhelming. Not for the first time, I found myself kinda feeling sorry for Alexa. "You said you saw her with someone," I said, jumping on that nugget of info. "Who was it?"

"Hell if I know."

"But you knew it was someone from the vampire parties?"

"Oh yeah," he said. "All dressed in goth black and had a pair of fangs in."

Which could have fit any one of the people we'd seen at the vampire party.

"Anything else you can tell us about him?" I asked, grasping.

He bit his lip, sucking a black stud into his mouth. "Yeah. The guy had these weird eyes. Like, super pale looking, you know?"

I did know.

Sebastian.

* * *

"So, Becca and Alexa are into something," I said, thinking out loud as we hopped back into Dana's Mustang. "Blackmail maybe. But something goes wrong, and Becca decides to kill Alexa. Only she needs help to stage it like a vampire murder."

"And she gets Sebastian to do it?" Dana asked.

"Or Darwin," I answered, playing devil's advocate. "I mean, we only have his word for it that Sebastian was even there."

"True," Dana nodded.

"Either way," I said, remembering what Goldstein had said about Becca being nervous, "the accomplice suddenly has the power, and now Becca is on the run."

"We've got to find her," Dana said.

I nodded. And quickly. Before the accomplice did.

"Well, the last place anyone saw her was in North Hollywood where Goldstein dropped her two nights ago."

"Let's check it out."

* * *

We stopped at a Jack-in-the-Box for a couple of sandwiches first (Okay, I had a couple of sandwiches, and Dana grilled the woman behind the counter to see if there was anything on the menu without trans fats and "hormone pumped meats", finally settling on a side salad sans dressing.), then we headed toward No Ho to look for Becca.

North Hollywood is not my favorite of places. First off, its name is deceiving. While Hollywood is known for glamour, glitz, and stars, North Hollywood is known for used cars (with or without pink slips), liquor stores, and porn studios. Bad place to drive at night, but a great place to hide out if you're on the run after killing your best friend.

We slowly drove down Victory, passing several sad storefronts and a couple of houses with tilting porches and chain link fences around the yards, until we hit Lankershim.

Dana pulled the Mustang in the lot of a strip mall featuring a discount cigarette shop, a check cashing place with bars on all the windows, and a pawn shop, and we took stock of the corner. Across from us was a furniture warehouse. On the opposite corner, a square cinderblock of cheap housing where a couple of guys in jeans that were just barely hanging onto their butts were engaging in pharmaceutical trade in the front entrance. Across the street from that sat a fast food place that served both Chinese and Mexican buffets all night long.

"Okay, so where do we think Becca is hiding out?" Dana asked, her eyes doing the same sweep as mine.

I shrugged. "The housing project?"

Dana nodded. "Likely place to start." She paused. "You wanna go in?"

I looked across at the Baggy Pants Dealers. I shook my head. "Not really."

"Yeah. Me neither."

We sat there for a beat, holding onto our chickenhood, watching the transaction complete across the street.

"Maybe we should drive around the back," Dana suggested. "Maybe just peek around. You know, with the windows up and the doors locked."

"Fabulous idea," I agreed.

We pulled back out onto the street, rounding Victory until we hit the back of the building. A small service alley separated it from the next block of houses behind it, the length of it filled with covered parking spots holding dented Chevy's, supped up Impalas, and a couple of vehicles so rusted they were beyond brand recognition. The pavement was coming up in chunks, the dumpsters overflowing, and the windows all covered in sheets and dirty blinds, shut tight against prying eyes.

Dana eased us down the length of the alley, passing by an emaciated looking dog and a group of boys with guilt written all over their faces. (I didn't even want to know why.) In the center of the building, the parking slots gave way to a small courtyard, punctuated with overgrown bushes and a couple of faded folding lawn chairs. An elderly man sat in one smoking a cigar in his boxers.

But there was no sign of Becca.

Dana swung into an empty spot at the end of the alleyway and, on a last ditch effort, I dialed Becca's cell number. I rolled my window down a crack, listening intently.

Through my phone I heard the call ringing on the other end. Outside the window all I heard was a dog barking somewhere far away and a booming bass from one of the upstairs apartments

"Even if she is around, we're not going to be able to hear her phone from in here," Dana pointed out.

I nodded. "Okay. Fine. We'll get out of the car."

I eyed the guilty looking kids. They wouldn't hurt a pregnant woman, right? I mean, they were just kids, right?

I slowly eased my car door open and gingerly stepped outside, immediately feeling like I was invading foreign territory. I heard Dana do the same, then quickly scuttle around to my side of the car, sticking close as I dialed Becca's number again. Again we waited, listening to it ring on my end. I closed my eyes, willing my hearing to strain to its most super sonic. I heard a baby crying somewhere inside the building. A muted TV show. And a faint ringing sound.

My eyes shot open. "I hear it!"

Dana must have heard it too, as I felt her perk up beside me. "Dial again," she prompted. "I think it was coming from that way." She pointed toward the middle of the alleyway where the building split in the center at the courtyard.

I did, hitting redial as we power walked toward the courtyard. This time the ringing on the other end grew louder as we approached. I turned into the courtyard, Dana a short step behind me. Bushes flanked either side of the tiny space, a cement block serving as a patio area. In the far right corner sat what might have been a koi pond in the building's finer years, but was now a concrete hole in the ground, covered by brush and debris.

The guy in the lawn chair watched us walk in.

"What you want?" he barked, smoke billowing from his mouth.

"Um, we're looking for our friend," I told him as the ringing went to voicemail on the other end. "Becca Diamond. Do you know her?"

The man stared at me. "What do I look like, the damned yellow pages?"

I bit my lip. "Right. Thanks. We'll just keep looking," I said, hitting redial again. I strained to hear which of the apartments the ringing on the other end might be coming from.

Only I realized, as I listened to it trill, that it didn't seem to be coming from the apartments above us. It seemed to be coming from somewhere below us.

"Maddie," Dana said, grabbing onto my arm. I looked up to see her staring at the koi pond.

Uh oh.

I took a step toward the abandoned pond. And heard the ringing grow louder. I slowly peered over the edge. It wasn't deep, only a couple of feet, though it was fully covered in palm fronds and trash.

And it was clearly ringing.

I bit my lip. I did an eenie meenie mine mo between curiosity and common sense. Ultimately, curiosity won out, and I gingerly reached down and shifted the palm fronds away from the edge of the pond.

What happened next was kind of a blur of "ohmigods", "holycraps", and high-pitched dog-whistle range screams. Some from Dana, but I'm pretty sure most were from me. Because staring back at us from the bottom of the abandoned koi pond were the lifeless blue eyes of Becca Diamond.

CHAPTER SIXTEEN

My hands were shaking as I dialed 911 and told the dispatcher what we'd just seen. Her calming tones did nothing to actually calm me down as she told me a squad car was on its way. Ten minutes later, it arrived, and the uniformed officer followed my shaking directions to the koi pond. Then he radioed in to dispatch for more squad cars. Twenty minutes later the entire block was filled with flashing red and blue lights, and the old man with the cigar and the kids had conspicuously disappeared inside.

Two officers split Dana and me up, an older redheaded guy taking Dana to one end of the courtyard to get her story and a younger guy with thick glasses taking me to the side closest to the alleyway.

"I understand you and your friend found the body?" he asked, pulling a notebook from his pocket.

I nodded, looking past him to where another squad car and the coroner's truck were pulling into the alleyway.

"Did you touch the body at all?"

I shook my head, nausea rolling through my stomach at the thought. "No way."

"But you could tell she was deceased?" he asked.

"Her eyes were open," I said. "And not moving."

He nodded. "Okay, what time exactly was this?"

I bit my lip. "I'm not sure. Maybe half an hour ago?" I said, watching as another car pulled into the alley behind us. A big, black SUV.

Uh oh.

"Um, do we really have to do this now?" I asked the officer. I watch the SUV park, a familiar figure emerging from the driver's side.

"Yes, ma'am. Now is a good time."

Maybe for him.

"Uh, okay, but you see I really have to…" I wracked my brain for an excuse to get away - any excuse! - as I watched Ramirez move away from his SUV to talk to another uniformed officer, no doubt being filled in on the fact that two ditzy blondes had found the body.

One of whom was conspicuously pregnant.

"…pee!" I yelled. I crossed my legs. "It's the pregnancy thing. The baby is sitting right on my bladder. Uncooperative little tyke. So, um, I have to go. Seriously. Now," I added with conviction as Ramirez's gaze swung my way. I ducked behind a tall bush, hoping The Bump didn't protrude too much.

"Oh, uh, well, I guess we could go to the station…" the officer said, his cheek turning pink as he stammered. Bad guys with guns he could handle. A pregnant woman with a small bladder, not so much.

Lucky for me.

"Yes, the station would be great. Wonderful. Perfect," I said. "I'm sure you have lovely bathrooms at the station. Shall we go now?" I turned and near-ran to the closest squad car as Ramirez entered the courtyard, his gaze sweeping over the scene, taking it all in. I could see his eyes were sharp, going into cop mode, making sure no little detail escaped him.

Even if she sorely wanted to.

"What's the hold-up?" I asked, slipping into the backseat of the car.

Officer Flustered took his sweet time closing his notebook, radioing in to someone that he was bringing in the witness for further questioning, mumbling a bunch of numbers and letters into the walkie attached to his belt.

Finally, after what seemed like an eternity, he got into the car and started the engine.

Not a moment too soon.

As he put the car into gear, I saw Ramirez's eyes lock in on Dana, gesturing wildly with her hands as the red-haired guy took her statement down as fast as he could scribble. Ramirez's jaw tightened, his eyes narrowed, and I thought I saw that little vein on the side of his neck start to pulse.

"Go! Drive!" I shouted, ducking down below the window panel.

Thankfully Officer Flustered did, pulling away from the curb just as a string of curses in Spanish emanated from my husband's mouth, following me down the street.

* * *

Once at the station I did, in fact, have to pee again so I hightailed it to the ladies room. Once relieved, I then sat with the uniformed officer and gave him a full statement. By the time he finally released me, I'd gone over our discovery at the koi pond about a hundred times and knew very detail of the moment like the back of my hand. The only thing I didn't know was what our murder*er* was doing murder*ed* in North Hollywood.

As soon as I left the station, I called Dana for a ride back home. Unfortunately there was no answer. She was probably still fending off the wrath of Ramirez. I totally owed her one. I made a mental note to take her out to the spa when this was all over. As a backup, I dialed Marco who, luckily, picked up on the third ring, did the appropriate amount of "ohmigod"s and "are you alright"s, then came to pick me up in his bright yellow Miata.

As reluctant as I was to face Ramirez, I knew from experience that the place he was least likely to be found after a dead body surfaced was home. So I took a chance and had Marco drop me off at my place with a promise that in the morning I'd fill him in on all the gory details of our finding.

I made myself a huge grilled cheese (Okay, I made two, but one was for the baby.), took the longest, hottest shower on record (which still didn't 100% get the feeling of dead person cooties off of me), and flopped into bed, willing myself to fall asleep before my husband got home.

Which, as it turned out, wasn't an issue. Since he didn't come home. A fact that left me with a mix of relief and dread in my stomach as I had brunch with Marco and Dana the next day at Café Melrose.

"I'm sure it was just because he was working," Marco said reassuringly as he sipped his mimosa.

I watched, sure I was turning green with envy. A mimosa would really hit the spot right about now.

"You think?" I asked, fiddling with the Denver omelet on my plate. "I mean, he seemed a little upset at the scene."

"A little?" Dana interjected. "I'm pretty sure people in Malibu heard him roaring about his little 'fregadita' of a wife."

Uh oh. Fregadita was his sometimes pet name for me that meant little pain in the ass. Only in this case, I'm pretty sure he didn't mean it as a term of endearment but more as an actual little pain in the ass.

"But he got over it, right?" I squeaked out hopefully.

Dana glared at me over her fat-free bran muffin. "If by 'over it' you mean he ranted for an hour, interrogated me for another hour, then cursed in Spanish for another hour, then yeah, he's totally over it."

I bit my lip. "Sorry. I totally owe you one. Honestly, I didn't think he'd take it out on you."

Dana shrugged. "I guess it could have been worse. At least it took my mind off of Ricky for a while."

"How is your Prince of Darkness lately?" Marco asked.

Dana sighed. "Don't ask. He was gone all night on another shoot with Ava. I swear to God if he signs on for another *Moonlight* movie next week, I may have to slit my wrists."

"Did he at least keep his phone on?" I asked.

Dana nodded. "Sure. In fact, he even accidentally butt-dialed me during the sex scene."

"Oh, no," I said, clucking my tongue in sympathy.

"Oh, yes. You know, it's one thing to know that your boyfriend is pretending to have sex with another girl, and it's another to actually have to hear it."

"What did you do?" Marco asked.

Dana bit her lip. "I hung up, then left him a couple of voicemails telling him to turn the phone off."

"A couple?" I asked.

Dana's cheeks went pink. "Okay, seventeen. Was that excessive?"

"Maybe just *this* much," Marco responded, holding up his thumb and forefinger.

Dana grabbed his mimosa and took a big gulp.

"Well, one thing's certain," I said, changing the subject before she downed the whole thing. "Clearly the fact that Becca is dead means she isn't our murderer."

Marco nodded. "Becca couldn't very well have murdered herself. So who did?"

"Okay, let's start at the beginning. Becca and Alexa were into something bad."

"Most likely blackmail ending in a big payout," Dana added.

"Right. They blackmail someone for cash, but something goes wrong and Alexa ends up dead. We thought Becca was on the run because she had something to do with Alexa's death, but what if it's the other way around? What if she was afraid for her life, too?"

"So she goes home and quickly grabs a bunch of clothes, then takes off," Marco added.

"But then why show up at the party the other night?" Dana asked. "Why not just take off for Mexico or something?"

I shoved a bite of omelet in my mouth, chewing thoughtfully. "Maybe she needed money? I mean, if their first attempt at blackmail failed, maybe she was broke. She needs some cash to get out of town, and now she has twice as much leverage against the blackmailee. She knows he killed Alexa."

Dana raised an eyebrow. "You think she'd be stupid enough to try blackmailing the guy again?"

I shrugged. "She didn't strike me as the brightest rhinestone on the ring, you know?"

Dana nodded. "Okay, so Becca goes in for a second blackmail attempt, but this one fails too, and instead of giving her the money the guy kills her."

"So, who is our blackmailee turned killer?" Marco asked.

"It must have been someone from the parties," I decided.

"So who was there that had a secret?" Marco asked.

I shrugged. "Who didn't? I mean I'm sure there are people who the very fact that they were at the parties was knowledge they wouldn't want to get out. Let alone the flirtations that went on there." I paused. "Or more than flirtations."

"I like Goldstein," Marco said. "He's rich, old, and married. Prefect material for blackmail."

"But what about Sebastian himself," Dana argued. "What if more was going on at those parties than we know about? What if he was pimping the girls out, and they got tired of it and tried to blackmail him for it?"

"But I don't think we should count out the boyfriend, either," I added. "He lied about knowing Alexa and he conveniently broke up with her right before she was killed. Or so he says."

"Plus he was at the club the night she died," Dana added.

"Let's face it, we have plenty of suspects," I said. "The problem is that we have absolutely no evidence."

"Goldstein was the last person to see Becca alive," Dana pointed out. "I think we need to talk to him again. Sure he *says* he dropped her off, but he could have easily killed her first."

I shrugged. "It's as good a place as any to start."

"Uh, I'm gonna let you gals go on ahead," Marco said, downing the last of his mimosa. "I've, uh, got somewhere to be this morning."

"A hot date?" I joked.

He grinned. "Something like that. I'll catch up with you ladies later, okay? Let me know how it goes with the lawyer," he said, then got up from the table and headed to the parking garage down the street.

I watched his retreating back. Hmm… Marco skipping out on a big interrogation? What was that boy up to?

*   *   *

An hour later Dana and I were hoofing it from the parking garage on 5th to Goldstein's corner office. We'd made it past the first receptionist, the second receptionist, and were just entering the third reception area when a familiar face began walking down the hallway toward us. Alexa's sister, Phoebe.

Her eyes were rimmed in red, and she was clutching a tissue in one hand. At her side was her husband, one hand on his wife's elbow, the other shoving a pair of spectacles back onto the bridge of his nose.

"Phoebe," I called.

She looked up, recognition struggling behind her eyes.

"Maddie Springer," I supplied. "We came to see you the other day about Alexa."

She nodded. "Yes, I remember you.

"What are you doing here?" I asked, looking past her down the hall as if the answer might materialize.

"We were making arrangements with our attorney."

"Wait," I said, my rusty mental wheels squeaking into action, "*Goldstein* is your attorney?" I asked.

She nodded. "Yes. He's handled all the family's affairs."

Mental forehead smack.

"He's helping us with the arrangements for Alexa's funeral," she added, her voice cracking on the last word, prompting the tissue to hit her cheeks.

"I'm so sorry," her husband said, putting an arm around his wife's shoulders. "But we've had a rough day. Do you mind?" he asked, brushing past us without waiting for an answer.

I watched them get onto the elevator, riding back down to reception number one.

"That's quite a coincidence," I mumbled.

"I'll say," Dana agreed. "The same guy who's sleeping with Becca *and* is the last person to see her alive *also* just happens to be Alexa's family lawyer. What are the chances?"

My thoughts exactly. "Let's go find out."

CHAPTER SEVENTEEN

"You didn't tell us that you knew Alexa before the parties," I said, once we had made it past receptionist number three and into Goldstein's inner offices.

Goldstein shook his head. "No, I didn't. It's called attorney-client privilege."

"So Alexa was your client?"

He paused. "I've been handling her family's affairs for some time. I mostly dealt with Phoebe, but I knew Alexa."

"That's what her sister told us," I said. "So you knew both Alexa and Becca slash Willow before you even started going to Sebastian's parties?"

He shook his head. "No, I knew Alexa. Becca I met at the parties."

"And that's when you started sleeping with her," Dana jumped in.

Goldstein shot her a look. "I'm sorry, but I don't have to answer any of your questions. And I don't particularly want to. So if you'll please excuse me," he said, gesturing toward his door.

But Dana wasn't giving up that easily. "Look, pal, you can either talk to us, or we can talk to you *wife*," she told him, leaving the threat hanging in the air.

Goldstein opened his mouth to protest, his cheeks going a deep red. But he must have seen the determination in Dana's eyes, as he shut his mouth again with a loud click. "Fine. Yes, Becca and I... spent time together. Becca was very special."

The use of the past tense told me that unlike Alexa, he had heard of Becca's passing. "We found her body yesterday," I told him.

His poker face slipped seamlessly into place. Whether he was saddened or relived by the fact that she was gone was a total mystery. "I heard," he said.

"She was killed in North Hollywood. Right where you dropped her off," I added.

"How horrible," came his monotone reply.

"Which means," I prompted, "that you were the last person to see her alive."

He paused, his eyes going from Dana to me. "Not quite," he countered. "Her *killer* would have been the last person to see her alive."

I raised an eyebrow his way. "Interesting distinction."

"An accurate one," he said, his meaning clear.

"Coincidental that she died right after you dropped her off."

Goldstein sat back in his chair, folding his hands over his stomach. "The police have determined the time of death?"

I paused. Honestly? I had no idea what the police had determined. I was kind of avoiding the police in general and one lead homicide detective specifically. "I'm not sure," I admitted.

"Well, you found her yesterday afternoon. That leaves a very large window of time from when I dropped her off the night before and when you found her. She could have been killed at any time."

Crap. This guy was good. I made a mental note to call him if I ever had any legal trouble.

I also silently decided it was time to get a peek at the M.E.'s report.

"When you dropped off Becca did you see anyone else around?" Dana asked, switching gears.

He paused. "There were a few people in the area."

"Any of them approach Becca? Anyone talk to her?"

"Not that I saw. It was dark, and I just dropped her off, then drove away."

"You dropped her off in a shady part of town, late at night, and just took off?" I asked.

He stared me down, and for a moment I had a horrible glimpse of what it would be like to face him across the witness stand.

"She asked me to drive her home," he said. "I drove her where she wanted to go. I didn't know she was going to be killed. Now if you'll excuse me," he said rising and gesturing to the open door.

Clearly that was all we were going to get from Mr. Courtroom. So, without much choice, we left.

"He seems guilty if you ask me," Dana said as we got in the elevator."

I nodded. "But guilty of what, is the question. Poor judgment? Adultery? Or murder?"

"All three?" Dana asked, shrugging her shoulders.

"What do you think Becca was doing in North Hollywood anyway?" I asked. "I mean, if she's running for her life, why not have him drop her off at the bus station or the airport?"

Dana nodded. "Good point. Maybe she knew someone in the building?"

I was just about to jump on that theory when the elevator dropped us off in the lobby, and Bill Blaise stepped toward us.

"We need to talk," he said, his voice low and urgent. I noticed that his wife was conspicuously absent this time.

"What is it?" I asked, as he ushered us to a quiet corner near a potted banana tree.

"This whole thing is very upsetting to my wife," he said.

I nodded. "I can understand why."

"She's feeling guilty for not having done enough for Alexa, even though I've told her we did all we could."

"I'm so sorry. I can only imagine," I said, honestly meaning it.

"The more questions the police ask, the worse it is for her," he continued. "What we need is to put this whole thing behind us and move on with our lives."

"Okay." I nodded again, not 100% sure where he was going with this.

"Once the funeral is over, I plan to take my wife on an extended vacation. Get her out of town, away from all this." He paused. "I'd really appreciate it if you could leave our family alone until then."

I raised an eyebrow his way. "Well, we came here to speak with Goldstein, not you and your wife."

He paused. "Goldstein. What does he have to do with this?"

I shifted, not entirely sure how much I should share.

"We think he may have been close to Becca. Alexa's friend."

His eyebrows furrowed together again. "The one they just found?"

I nodded. "He was the last person to see her alive."

"And you think he may have had something to do with her death?" he asked, leaning in close. "And Alexa's?"

"We're really not sure," I hedged. "We're just gathering information at this point."

He took this all in, his eyes unreadable. "I see. Well, like I said, I'd really appreciate it if you would keep my wife out of it all. I..." he paused, genuine emotion showing behind his eyes. "I just don't want to see her hurt anymore."

"I understand," I said.

"Thank you," he said. He pursed his lips together, then nodded at both Dana and I before turning away.

But as I watched him walk across the lobby then push through the glass front doors of the building, I couldn't help but wonder just how much of that speech had been about protecting his wife and how much had been about discerning what we'd just pulled from Goldstein.

* * *

"I'm starving," I said as we got back into Dana's Mustang. "Any chance we could go grab a burger?"

Dana bit her lip. "Actually, I think we should be getting home."

"Please, just a quick one?" I pleaded. "I'll get it to go?"

"Let's eat at your place," Dana protested, getting on the 101.

I felt my forehead wrinkling. "Why?"

"Weeell… I just have some stuff to do this afternoon."

"Stuff?"

"Uh huh."

"What kind of stuff?"

"You know." She shrugged. "Stuff."

"O-kay," I responded. "Fine. Let's go to my place. But hurry. I kinda have to pee."

* * *

Once we pulled up to my house, Dana parked in the drive and followed me up the pathway to the front door. I stuck my key in, turned the knob, pushed through the front doors… and was immediately assaulted by dozens of pink and blue balloons.

"Surprise!" about fifteen different people yelled, jumping out from my kitchen. Among them I spotted my mom, Mrs. Rosenblatt, my cousin, Molly, and Marco and his Norwegian bodybuilder, Gunnar.

I blinked. Oh lord. I didn't know what this was, but it couldn't be good.

Marco jumped forward, grabbing me in a big bear hug. "Did you know? Did we surprise you? Your mom said for sure you'd know, but I said, 'No way, she'll be totally surprised.'"

"I'm totally surprised," I promised him. "What is this?"

"Your baby shower," Mom said, coming in for a hug of her own.

I blinked, my eyes going around the room. "Wow, that's really… wow," I said, taking in the decorations. My living room had been entirely transformed into a sea of pink and blue streamers. Cardboard baby bottles, pacifiers and carriages had been plastered on every square inch of wall space. And in the center of the room stood a six foot tall, plastic stork.

I turned to find Dana grinning behind me.

"Did you know about this?" I asked.

She nodded, pure white teeth smiling from ear to ear.

"And you didn't warn me?"

She shrugged. "It was surprise."

"I'm totally interviewing for a new best friend," I mumbled to her as Marco grabbed my right hand, Mom grabbed my left, and together they dragged me to a chair set under the stork.

"Presents," Mom instructed my cousin, Molly. "She's in shock. She needs a present!"

A second later a package wrapped in yellow paper was thrust into my lap, fifteen eager eyes turned my way, as Mom instructed, "Open it."

"This one's from me," Molly said. Molly had four kids, short brown hair cut into a Tipper Gore bob, and a mini-van with at least a box and a half of Cheerios shoved down the seats. Molly was all my greatest fears about motherhood wrapped into one loafer-wearing package.

I carefully pulled the paper back, lifted the lid of the cardboard box beneath, and pulled out a cone-shaped thing covered in little blue teddy bears.

I held it up, raising an eyebrow at Molly.

"It's a Peepee Teepee!" she proudly exclaimed.

"A what?"

"You put it on a baby boy's wee-wee so that he doesn't shoot you in the eye with pee-pee while you're changing his diaper," she explained.

I looked down at the cone. "Does that actually happen?"

Molly laughed. "All the time."

Another great reason to cross my fingers for a girl.

"Mine next," Mom said, thrusting a package at me covered in little green boats.

I pulled at the tissue, digging around inside the bag, and came out with what looked like a tiny, blue straightjacket.

"What's this?" I asked, that familiar bubble of panic settling in as I realized I didn't know what *any* of this stuff was.

"A baby carrier!" my mom announced, taking it from my hands and proceeding to wrap it around my middle. "Now you can have your baby strapped to you wherever you go."

"Actually, I'm really kind of looking forward to *not* carrying a baby around on my belly," I protested as she continued to strap me in.

"You'll love this," she said, completely ignoring me. "You can have you hands free this way."

"Can't I just put the baby down and have my hands free?"

Mom stopped strapping and looked at me in horror.

"I'd put her down gently," I promised.

But she just clucked her tongue at me.

About a hundred straps later, Mom was done, and I had what looked like a kangaroo pouch strapped to my front.

Mom reached into my Santana bag, grabbed Baby-So-Lifelike, and shoved the vinyl doll into the pouch. "There! A perfect fit!"

I opened my mouth to protest, but didn't get a chance.

"The games are ready!" Marco announced, clapping his hands together. "Everyone come out to the backyard. We have some fabu party games ready!"

Reluctantly, I followed, trying (without much luck) to wiggle out from the straightjacket's grasp as I made my way into the backyard.

California real estate being worth what it was, yards in L.A. were generally small patches of semi-green (thanks to our perpetual droughts) grass. But Ramirez had made the best use possible of our small outdoor space, building a stone patio to one side of the lawn, which was at present filled with rows of tables clad in bright yellow tablecloths. Covered in yellow ducks. Wearing yellow baby bonnets. In the center of each one was a metal baby carriage overflowing with pink and blue flowers.

"Maddie, you sit here," Marco said, indicating a spot at the head of one table. "We're going to play Name That Food."

Okay, now we were getting somewhere. Food was good. I didn't dare hope he was bringing out burgers, but my growling stomach wasn't in the mood to be too picky right about now.

"Everyone take a seat," Marco instructed. "I'm handing out plates of baby food. Your mission is to taste each one, then guess as many flavors correctly as you can."

Mom took a spot next to me, Gunnar taking the one on the other side and Molly sitting beside him as Marco set down paper plates with several little piles of colorful mush on each.

I sniffed at the plate. Okay, whoever called this "food" had a loose interpretation of the word. I gingerly stuck my finger in a pile of purple mush and tasted it on the tip of my tongue.

Huh, not so bad, actually. Plum if I had to guess. I wrote my answer down on the yellow notepad Marco had provided, then moved on to the next pile.

This one was orange. I stuck my finger in and gave it a lick.

Then immediately regretted it.

I wrote "chicken vomit" on my pad.

I hesitantly tried the next pile, a pale green one. It was a cross between cold pea soup and kindergarten paste.

I made a mental note to never feed my child this. It was tantamount to child abuse.

After completely failing at the baby food test (the answers were Prunes, Chicken and Rice, and Peas and Carrots), Marco brought out the next game.

"Baby Jeopardy!" he announced. "I'll call out a question, and the first person to shout out the answer, in the form of a question," he added, "wins. Everyone ready?"

I sat up straighter in my chair. I had read *What to Expect When You're Expecting* at least three times, cover to cover. I'd even memorized the first two chapters of *What to Expect the First Year*. This one I could do.

"What," Marco asked, reading off of a little yellow index card, "is the age at which babies first learn to crawl?"

"What is two!" I shouted out.

Mom turned to me. "Years?"

I bit my lip. "Um… months?" I said, though it came out more of a question.

Mom looked down at Baby-So-Lifelike with something akin to sympathy in her eyes.

"Sorry, that's incorrect," Marco said shaking his head. "Anyone else?"

My cousin, Molly, raised her hand. "According to the American Academy of Pediatricians, most babies hit that developmental milestone between the ages of six and ten months. So, what is six to ten months?"

"Correct!" Marco said. "Very impressive honey. One point for the woman with the fabu bob."

Molly preened in her seat.

"No fair," I mumbled under my breath. "I haven't gotten to that chapter yet."

"Next question," Marco announced. "At what age do babies get their first tooth?"

I wisely stayed silent on this one, letting my cousin, Molly, shout out an answer again. "Most pediatricians agree that children will get their first deciduous tooth between the ages of four and seven months."

"Correct!" Marco said. "But you didn't phrase it in the form of a question."

Molly's face fell.

"Okay, next question. How long do most pediatricians recommend you breastfeed your baby?"

"What is twelve months!" Mrs. Rosenblatt shouted out this time.

"Correct!" Marco said. "One point for the lady in the fashionable muumuu!"

"Wait," I said, leaning toward my mom. "Didn't he just say that babies get their first teeth at four months?"

Mom nodded.

"And then we breastfeed for another eight months?"

She nodded again.

My nipples cringed. Suddenly feeding The Bump pea-puke baby food didn't sound like such a bad idea after all.

CHAPTER EIGHTEEN

―――

Three hours, two party games, and one cake shaped like a stork later, I was just cleaning up the last of the balloons when Ramirez walked through the front door. He stopped dead in his tracks, staring at the mounds of pink and blue colored tissue paper.

"Surprise baby shower," I explained. "So not my idea."

He walked over to the pile of baby gifts leaning precariously against the sofa. "We get anything good?"

"A Boppy, a Bumpo, and a Tommee Tippee gift basket." I paused. "I don't know what any of those things are."

Ramirez grinned. "I like your new look," he said gesturing to my torso.

I glanced down and realized Baby-So-Lifelike was still attached to me. Oddly enough, I had kind of forgotten about her. Maybe the carrier wasn't such a bad thing after all.

"Mom said I need practice."

He nodded. "Good idea. I remember the ficus."

I rolled my eyes. "Geeze, it was one little plant."

"Three, if I recall."

"I'm practicing, okay," I said, gesturing to the doll strapped to my mid-section. I paused. "So, you gonna start with the yelling now?" I asked.

Ramirez let out a long sigh, then sank into the sofa. "I probably should. It's getting late, and we have a lot of ground to cover."

"Very funny," I countered, sinking into the sofa beside him. Though, the fact he was teasing me was a good sign. "You know it's not my fault, right? I mean, we just found her like that."

Ramirez shot me a look. "Uh huh. And what were you doing there in the first place?"

"Nothing," I said, though I noticed my voice rose about an octave. "We just wanted to talk to Becca, that's all."

"Instead you found her dead body."

"Sorta?"

"And," he added, "your prints were found all over her apartment. You want to explain that?"

I bit my lip. "Not really."

"Maddie…"

"Okay, I was at her place the other day. The door was unlocked, so we kind of stepped inside. And maybe looked around a little. But Becca wasn't there, I swear it."

He ran a hand over his face. "You know, between the death threat you gave Alexa and the fingerprints at Becca's, it's becoming a full time job convincing my captain that my wife isn't involved in these murders."

I bit my lip again. "Sorry?"

He shot me the look again.

"Really, really sorry?" I amended.

He let out another deep sigh. "Just stay away from my crime scene from now on, capiche, Springer?"

I nodded. "Capiche. So, we're cool?" I asked.

He gave me a tired smile. "We're fine, Maddie."

Fine. Not exactly the most passionate term to describe a relationship. But I figured at the moment fine was the best I could hope for.

"I've got some reports to go over tonight," he told me, getting up from the sofa. "Any party leftovers?" he asked hopefully.

"There's the stork beak still left on the cake."

He grinned. "Perfect," he said, then ducked into the kitchen with his briefcase full of papers.

Though, for once, I didn't mind being neglected in favor of paperwork. Because if those reports were what I thought they were, I fully intended to do a little paperwork of my own the second he left them unattended.

* * *

"Flunitrazepam," I told Dana and Marco the next day in the reception area of Fernando's salon.

"Fluniwhatnow?" Marco asked.

"Ruffies," Dana supplied. "Date rape drug."

I nodded. "That's what was in Becca's system. A whole lot of it, according to the M.E.'s report that I read last night. Enough to put down an elephant, let alone a hundred pound woman."

"So, whoever killed Becca drugged her to death?" Marco asked.

"And also drugged Alexa," I added, triumphantly. "After Ramirez fell asleep I snuck a peek at her report, too. We were right. She was drugged first, then drained of blood."

"Which explains why she didn't struggle," Dana added.

"And, also why there was no blood at the scene. Flunitrazepam inhibits blood pressure, so it would have been easy to puncture her neck, lean her over the toilet, then let her blood drain and flush it away."

"Assuming he didn't drink it," Marco put in.

Dana and I did the simultaneous eye roll thing again. We were getting pretty good at it. Almost completely synchronized this time.

"Okay, so the killer drugs Alexa, kills her, then the night of the party he follows Becca and drugs her, too?" Dana asked.

I shook my head. "No. That's the genius part. I did a little googling and found out that the drug doesn't kick in until a full thirty minutes after the victim ingests it, and it doesn't take full effect until two hours afterward."

"So whoever killed her must have spiked her drink at the party," Marco said.

I pointed at him. "Bingo. All he had to do was make sure she drank the stuff, then he'd likely be nowhere near the body at the time she actually died."

"So it was Sebastian!" Marco said. "I knew it."

"Goldstein was at the party, too," Dana pointed out.

"Yeah, but what are the chances he'd drug her, providing himself with a great alibi, then actually drive her somewhere and wait to watch her die? It defeats the purpose of using the time-released drug."

I nodded. "Good point. Okay, so let's assume that it was Sebastian. Let's say the girls were blackmailing him over something that happened at the parties, and he kills Alexa at the club, making it look like one of her vampire-wanna-be lovers did her in."

"Then when Becca comes nosing around for pay-off money to keep quiet about the murder, he spikes her drink," Marco continued, "knowing that by the end of the night, she'll be dead, too."

"Perfect!" Dana agreed. "Now all we have to do is prove it."

"What we need is to find the murder weapon," I decided.

"Uh, Mads? The guy's fangs are in his mouth," Marco pointed out.

I shot him a look. "I meant the drug. He clearly kept it around after he killed Alexa. Maybe he's still got some squirreled away somewhere now."

"And, if so," Dana said, "it's probably at his place right now."

"Which means we need to find it, quickly, before he gets rid of the evidence."

"So we break into his place?" Dana asked.

I shook my head. "We don't need to. I called the girls' agent, Bowman, and he said that Sebastian is having another party tonight."

"Perfect!" Dana said.

Marco did a deep sigh. "Fine. But we need to swing by my place after work so I can change into my turtleneck."

CHAPTER NINETEEN

———

We left Marco to finish his shift at Fernando's, promising we'd pick him and his turtleneck up later that evening. Then Dana went back to the Sunset Studios lot to score us more vampire attire and three pairs of fangs, and I went home to a) pee and b) eat. Only the second I walked in the door I was ambushed by my mother and Mrs. Rosenblatt.

"Why is my grandchild home alone again?" Mom asked, pouncing on me as she cradled Baby-So-Lifelike in her arms.

I looked down at my Santana bag. Crap. I'd forgotten to take the doll out of the carrier last night.

"Sorry. I forgot," I mumbled, pushing past her toward the hall bathroom.

"Forgot?" her voice followed me. "You can't just forget a baby, Maddie!"

I shut the door, giving my eyes a good three-sixty the second I was out of her sight. "I forgot the *doll*. I won't forget a real baby."

"You are failing at practice, young lady!" she shouted.

I ignored her, instead moving to do my business. But as I looked down at the toilet seat, I realized that wasn't going to be possible. There was a bulky plastic arm wedged between the tank and the lid, holding it firmly shut. I tried lifting it, but it wouldn't budge.

"Mom?" I called, reopening the bathroom door. "Did you do something to my toilet?"

She appeared in the doorway a moment later. "Yes. I locked it."

"Is this some sort of punishment?" I asked, crossing my legs.

"Oh for goodness sakes, Maddie," Mom chided. "It's for the baby. You can't have him playing in the toilet water. And you and Ramirez didn't have *anything* baby proofed yet. Mrs. Rosenblatt and I thought we'd come over and help."

"You know what would help?" I asked. "If you'd unlock my toilet."

She gave me a look, but thankfully did, pushing some button, pulling some lever, and twisting some piece of plastic until the lid popped open.

I quickly shooed her out of the room and did my thing, emerging a new woman a few minutes later.

Where I saw Mom and Mrs. R fiddling with another suspicious looking piece of plastic on the refrigerator door.

Oh no.

"Uh, what else have you two baby proofed around here?" I asked, my eyes whipping around the living area.

"Just the basics," Mom assured me. Then proceeded to tick off items on her fingers. "Locks on the bathroom cabinets, safety rubber on the bathtub faucet, door stoppers and handle locks on all the doors, an oven shield, bumpers on the fireplace and all of the table corners, outlet covers, power strip covers, a baby gate for the kitchen doorway, and a refrigerator lock."

I blinked at her. Then blinked at my living room. It was covered in soft foam and white plastic contraptions. "Do we really need *all* of this?"

"That depends," My mom said, putting both hands on her hips. "Do you want your child to be safe?"

"Fine, okay," I conceded. "I'll find a way to rock the padded cell look. Though I do have one teeny tiny favor to ask?"

"Yes?"

"Any chance I could get a sandwich from the refrigerator before you lock it up?"

* * *

I spent the rest of the afternoon nibbling, napping, and putting the finishing touches on the white woven wedge for my spring collection – generally trying to take my mind off our evening of snooping around a killer's house. Which didn't work all that well, as by the time Dana arrived on my doorstep that evening I was a bundle of nerves anyway. (But I was proud to say the wedges were looking hot!)

Dana had managed to commandeer another pair of gothic style outfits from the set, and she quickly helped me into mine. It was a deep burgundy jacket in crushed velvet with black lace peeking out from the collar and sleeves, paired with a long black skirt. It came with a "loose" blouse, but after popping one of the buttons, it was clear I wasn't going to be able to fit in it. Instead, I grabbed a black, long sleeve work-out T from my closet, dressing it up with an oversized crucifix my Irish Catholic grandmother had given me when I'd started dating Ramirez.

Dana had gone the slinky route again, wearing a short, black, satin dress that dipped low in the front, showing off an Elvira-worthy amount of cleavage. It was the perfect disguise; I could guarantee no man would be able to remember her face. She'd paired it with a long, black cape, high platform shoes, and a long, dark wig that perfectly matched mine.

We both capped off the outfits with a pair of fake fangs, attached with some Fixodent she'd picked up at the drug store.

We were just putting the finishing touches on our smoky eyes and ruby-red lips when my doorbell rang. I opened it to find Marco standing on the other side.

He'd done his own version of gothic chic with a pair of black leather pants, a fitted turtleneck shirt and black boots. He'd gone double thick with the eyeliner tonight, and over his shoulder he'd slung a big leather bag.

"Let's do this," he said by way of greeting, stepping into the room.

I sniffed the air as he walked past me. "Did you have garlic for dinner?" I asked.

"No. I rubbed raw cloves all over my body," he informed me. "Just in case."

I rolled my eyes. "They're not real," I told him for the millionth time.

"Says you."

"Dana?" I called for backup.

"Hey, it never hurts to be prepared," Marco argued. "In fact, I've got a whole satchel of vampire hunting items here," he said, digging into his bag.

I had to admit, morbid curiosity won me over. "Like what?" I asked, leaning forward.

"Rosary beads, of course. And a bible," he said, pulling out a pocket sized version. "And then just the essentials for killing vampires," he said, more items coming out of his bag.

I looked down at a dozen wooden kabob skewers, a bottle of Evian, and a can of tanning spray. I looked up at Marco and gave him the raised eyebrow. "And these are deadly how?"

Marco rolled his eyes at me. (Yeah, seriously. The guy in leather pants that smelled like an Italian restaurant thought I was crazy.) "Uh, hello? Wooden stake to the heart, holy water, and sunlight. The trinity of vampire hunting."

I picked up the bottled water. "Evian?"

Marco shrugged. "Gunnar said a Nordic prayer over it. It was the best I could do on short notice."

"And tanning spray?"

"What? It says 'sunshine in a can' on the label."

"Okay, are we ready?" Dana asked, emerging from the bathroom, eyes super smoky.

"Almost," Marco said. "I was nervous, so I drank the other bottle of Evian on the way over. Can I use the little boys' room?"

I pointed down the hallway. "Be my guest."

"Gracias," he called after himself as he skipped toward it.

"What is all this stuff?" Dana asked looking down at Marco's slayer kit.

"You don't want to know," I told her, fairly confident it was true.

"Maddie?" I heard from the bathroom. "Help!"

Dana and I made our way to the door to find Marco bent over the toilet, his legs crossed. "I can't get this lock thingie off," he whimpered.

Oh, brother. I leaned down and looked at the plastic contraption that my mom had installed, trying to remember how she'd worked it earlier. There was a button, a lever, a little red indicator window, and a latch. I pushed the button. Nothing. I flipped the latch, and the indicator turned green, but the lid was still securely stuck. I pushed the button and flipped the latch. Nada.

"Ohmigod, I'm gonna pee my pants," Marco whined dancing from foot to foot.

"Go use the other bathroom," I said, gesturing to the master.

Marco bolted, running down the hallway as quickly as a man crossing his legs could.

"Maybe you need to move the lever?" Dana suggested.

I tried that, and the indicator turned red again.

"Maybe move the lever and flip the latch?" she said, doing just that. But the lid didn't move.

"Did this thing come with instructions?" she asked.

"This one's locked, too!" Marco screamed from the master bathroom. "I'm gonna burst!"

"Wow, your mom is really taking this baby safety things seriously. I'm impressed," Dana said, nodding.

"Hurry, oh God, please hurry!" Marco yelled, pee-pee dancing back down the hallway. "These pants are Versace, and I'm two seconds away from tinkling on them!"

"Okay, we can do this," I said, staring the gadget down. We were three smart, educated, intelligent people. More importantly, we were all over the age of two. We would conquer the baby proof lock.

I moved the lever, flipped the latch and pushed the button. Nothing. I pushed the button, moved the lever, then flipped the latch. Nada.

"Ohmigod. My bladder. She's gonna burst."

"You have a female bladder?" Dana asked, giggling.

"Shut up. Don't make me laugh!" Marco commanded.

"Wait, I think I got it," I said, feeling the tip of my tongue protrude from my mouth in extreme concentration. I flipped the latch, moved the lever, pushed the button and watched in awe as the little indicator window turned green and the lock fell away in my hand.

"My hero," Marco yelled, pushing me out of the way and unzipping his pants all in one motion.

Dana and I jumped out of the bathroom, barely getting the door closed before the sound of Niagara Falls hit our ears.

"Oh, sweet mother of all that is liquid, that is heaven," Marco moaned from the other side of the door.

Well, as long as my baby wasn't any smarter than Marco, I guess she'd be safe.

* * *

We managed to arrive at Sebastian's without further incident and parked in the circular drive beside the other party-goers' cars. Marco shoved his hand in his satchel, clutching his rosary beads as we entered through the large, wooden, front doors, the sounds of music and laughter washing over us.

The scene was much like the one Dana and I had witnessed the last time we'd crashed Sebastian's party. Men and women dressed in all manner of black attire sipped drinks, chatting in groups, while a few couples made out in the shadows. Minus the bloodsucking undertones, it was just like any other party in the Hollywood Hills that night.

Only a killer was hosting this one.

"I say we start in Sebastian's bedroom," I suggested, gesturing up the winding staircase. "It's the most likely place he'd hide something personal."

Dana nodded. "Agreed."

Marco followed a step behind as we ascended the stairs, brushing past a couple of women in short skirts, long wigs, and gleaming oversized canines. We hit the top landing, then quickly made our way to the master suite Dana and I had found on our earlier trip. I did an over the shoulder, making sure we were alone, then gently turned the knob. Luckily, it moved easily in my hand and a second later we were inside the vampire's private lair.

"This is so creepy," Marco said, eyes darting around the room as if searching for signs of bats and coffins.

"It's just some guy's bedroom," I told him. Though I wasn't entirely comfortable with being there either. Even if Sebastian was just some guy, he was a guy who'd killed two women. The sooner we were out of here with the evidence, the better.

"I'm going to take the bathroom," I informed my friends, moving to the far end of the room.

I passed through a doorway into a bathroom that was as big as my entire house. Sleek black marble covered the floors while contrasting, white, subway tiles lined the walls. The counters were a dark stone, supporting two clear, vessel sinks. It was more modern than I would have envisioned for a gothic vampire, but I supposed it suited a fake one.

In the absence of an obvious medicine cabinet, I started opening drawers, looking for anything that could be a vial of date-rape drugs. I found a shocking amount of hair products, several toothbrushes, including one very sophisticated electric one, and a healthy supply of whitening strips.

But no murder weapon.

I moved on to the cupboards beneath, coming up with the usual assortment of cleaning supplies. Nothing out of the ordinary or, honestly, very different than what was in my own bathroom cabinets. (Not that I could get into them anymore.)

"Any luck?" I heard Dana call from the other room.

I ducked my head back out. "No. You guys?"

"Nothing," Dana informed me. "We checked the closets, drawers, under the bed. There are no drugs anywhere."

I pursed my lips together. This was starting to look like another fruitless investigation.

"This house is huge," Marco said. "Maybe he hid it in another room?"

I shrugged. "It's definitely worth looking."

We quietly slipped from Sebastian's room, back out into the hallway. I'm sure guilt was etched on each of our faces as a couple came up the stairs, the woman giggling and laughing at something the guy in another long, black wig said, but they seemed too engrossed in each other to notice us.

As soon as they passed us, Marco hissed, "Where to now?"

I looked down the hallway. Six closed doors stared back at me, three on either side.

"I say we split up," I decided. "It's the fastest way to search everything before someone finds us here."

Marco bit his lip. He stuck his hand in his bag again, fingering his rosary beads. He took a deep breath and adjusted his turtleneck. "Okay. I can do this."

We split off, each of us taking a separate door. Mine turned out to be a library of sorts, books lining the walls all the way to the ceiling on one side. Two large, leather chairs took up the center of the room, while a giant globe sat in the corner against the windows. It had an oddly old-world feel that contrasted with the modern look in the rest of the house.

Luckily, though, it was rather sparsely furnished, making my job easier.

I quickly looked through the few built-in cabinets beside the globe and shuffled a few books looking for any sort of secret hiding places, before ascertaining that the room was clean.

I was beginning to worry that maybe Sebastian had disposed of the evidence this time after all.

I crossed back to the door and put my ear to the wooden panel, listening for voices. Nothing. The hallway was clear. I quickly opened it, slipped outside, and casually walked to the room next door.

This one was dark, the lights shut off. But in the shadows I could make out a double bed and a small dresser. A guest room, if I had to guess. While light would have made searching a whole lot easier, the windows of this room faced directly onto the circular front drive. Anyone down below would have seen it go on. So instead I blinked, adjusting my eyes to the darkness as I felt in front of me toward the dresser.

I quickly went through the drawers, coming up with only spare linens, then began running my hands under the pillow and sheets for anything that felt cold, metal, or lethal.

I was just about to give up, having ascertained that the mattress did not have any secrets stashed under it, when I heard the door open.

I froze, ducking down behind the bed.

"Maddie?" a voice whispered, though it was so low I couldn't tell whether it was Dana or Marco.

"Over here," I said, relief flooding through me as I stood up.

Though I soon realized that the relief was premature.

And that the voice had belonged to neither Marco nor Dana. Because I knew for a fact that neither one of them would have raised their arm above their body as I watched the shadowy figure do, clutching something dark and heavy in one hand, then bring it down on the side of my head with such force that I fell to the ground.

I got a great view of the dust bunnies living under Sebastian's guest bed for a half a second before I felt my eyelids fall forward, plunging me into darkness.

CHAPTER TWENTY

When I had found out I was pregnant, the first thing I did (after having a mild panic attack) was google what sort of delicious things I could now not consume. I knew alcohol was definitely out, but I was surprised to find that soft cheese, raw eggs, and certain fish were also on the list. Along with my biggest indulgence – coffee. I'm pretty sure people all the way in Riverside County heard my sobs when I realized it was nine months of no Starbucks for me. And the first day I had gone zero caffeine, cold turkey down from my usual three-lattes-a-day habit, I'd had a caffeine deprivation headache so horrible I'd thought that my head might actually explode. My temples throbbed, my eyes burned, and my head felt twice its usual size.

But that, I realized as I slowly blinked one eye open, was nothing compared to how my head felt now.

I heard myself moan as I slowly managed to get both eyes open, blinking in the darkness. I wasn't sure where I was, but it was cold and moist, the air was damp in a way that instantly made me have to pee. And it was pitch black. Not a sliver of light shone anywhere. I continued blinking, fighting through the throbbing pain with each miniscule movement of my eyelids, as I tried to get my eyes to adjust to the absence of light. I gingerly moved my fingers, hands, legs. All seemed to be in working order, though I could feel stiffness settling in my limbs. I had no idea how long I'd been unconscious. Or, for that matter, who'd made me that way.

"Hello?" I called out in a voice that could have belonged to a scared two year old.

I thought I heard a faint rustling sound to my right in response.

I moved toward it. "Hello? Is anyone there?" I asked, not sure if I wanted someone to be or not. The last person I'd seen had hit me on the head. Not exactly ideal company.

I heard more rustling, this time accompanied by a moan much like the one I'd just made.

"Maddie?" a small, female voice called out.

"Dana! Is that you?" I asked, reaching my hands out in front of me as I slowly moved toward the sound.

"My head is killing me," Dana whined, her voice growing closer as I carefully crawled along the floor toward her.

"What happened?" I asked.

"I don't know. One minute I was searching through a bathroom cabinet, the next I'm here." She paused. "Are you okay?"

I nodded in the dark. "Yeah. Ditto the headache, but I'm alright," I said, feeling my hands come up against the fabric of her satin dress. She quickly grabbed my hand, squeezing it in hers as if she expected the Boogieman to jump out at us any second.

Which, honestly, was a possibility at this point.

"Where's Marco?" I asked.

"I don't know. He took the next door down from me."

"Marco?" I called out in the darkness.

But only silence echoed back at me.

I felt Dana squeeze my hand just that much tighter.

"I'm sure he's okay," I said, more to myself than her. "I'm sure he's fine, he's looking for us, maybe even going for help right now."

I felt Dana nod beside me. "Uh huh," she agreed. Though her voice was about as unconvincing as mine. "Any clue where we are?" Dana asked

I shook my head. (Which, by the way was a very bad idea, prompting more throbbing, burning, and general pain in my temples.) "None," I answered, truthfully. I squinted through the blackness, my eyes having adjusted just enough to make out some basic shapes. We were in a corridor of some kind, only a few feet wide but long enough that I couldn't see the end of it. The walls were concrete, the same cold, damp consistency as the floor. I could hear the faint sounds of music and laughter, telling me the head-basher hadn't dragged us too far from Sebastian's party. I swiveled around and could just make out the shape of a doorway behind me.

"Look over there," I said, pointing it out.

I slowly stood up, realizing my left foot was asleep, and waddled toward it. I felt Dana right behind me, her hands on my back as she felt her way along the damp walls. Unfortunately, as we got closer, I realized that, while it was a door alright, there was no handle on our side of it.

I ran my fingers along the edges, looking for any sort of spot to get a finger-hold, but came up empty.

Dana hit the door with her palm. "Hey!" she shouted. She did some more pounding. "Help! Can anyone hear us?"

Only silence greeted us on the other side.

If we were still hidden away somewhere at Sebastian's place, the party music was too loud for anyone to hear us.

I spun around, instead scanning the corridor for anything we might be able to use to pry the door open. Sadly, I could only see about a foot in front of myself. I squatted down, slowing crawling along the floor, hands out in front of me, hoping they contacted with something useful before they contacted with something yucky. Dust, a cobweb (definitely yucky!), and more damp floor. I was about to give up when my hands hit something soft and leathery. I grabbed on, exploring the surface and coming up against fringe before I realized it was my Santana bag!

"Dana, my purse is in here," I shouted, feeling her come up behind me. I dug my hands inside, feeling the vinyl arms of Baby-So-Lifelike, the cold metal of a lipstick tube, a couple of tampons long forgotten in the bottom, some receipts, and a few pieces I couldn't identify by touch. The one thing noticeably absent was my cell.

I felt my spirits sinking faster than the Titanic. "He took my phone."

"Same here," I heard Dana say, rustling to my right. "He left a nail file, though. Think that might help?"

"It's worth a try."

We held hands, feeling our way in the dark back toward the knob-less door, and stuck the metal file into the crack between the door and the jamb. Dana wiggled it, twisted it, moved it up and down.

But the door stayed shut.

I'm not sure how long we stood there jiggling, but my right foot was just starting to join my left in dreamland when I heard a sound on the other side of the door.

I froze.

I felt Dana go still beside me. She'd heard it too.

We both jumped back, and I bit my lip, uncertain if I should try to hide or call for help.

"Help!" Dana yelled, apparently not having the same dilemma. "Someone help! We're stuck in here!" she yelled.

A second later the door swung open, the sudden light blinding me. Instinctively I ducked my head, shielding my eyes from the onslaught of brightness.

"Marco!" I heard Dana yell beside me.

I blinked against the light, making out two forms silhouetted in the doorway. One was slumped forward, limp as a ragdoll, and wearing skintight pants. The other was tall, holding form number one up, and holding a gun in the other hand.

I did an involuntary yip that echoed in the corridor as the form with the gun unceremoniously dumped Marco at our feet.

"Marco, can you hear me?" Dana asked, quickly crawling toward him.

"Don't move," the figure holding the gun informed her.

Dana froze.

"Either of you," he said, swinging the weapon my way.

I wisely froze, too.

The figure reached behind himself and shut the door again, closing off any means of escape, then switched on a flashlight, bathing the room in soft light.

I looked up at our attacker, expecting to see icy blue eyes and a pair of fangs gleaming at me.

Instead, I saw a thick head of hair, thick glasses, and a thick dimpled neck.

Bill Blaise.

I blinked, feeling a frown form between my eyebrows as I took in his black slacks, black jacket, and costume-store fangs. "I don't understand," I mused out loud. "What are you doing here?"

He turned the gun my way. "What am I doing here? What are *you* doing here, is the question," he countered. "What are you doing nosing around where you don't belong. Stirring up trouble where there was none. Digging into people's personal lives that should be left alone."

Honestly? I did have a habit of doing that. But I didn't think now was the time to admit it.

"Against the wall," he said, motioning Dana and I to the far side of the corridor.

We scuttled backward, crab-walking until I felt the concrete of the wall hit my back.

"You killed Alexa?" I asked, puzzle pieces slowly falling into place.

He spun on me. "Brilliant, Sherlock," he said, heavy on the sarcasm.

"But why?"

"Why? Because the bitch was blackmailing me, that's why," he spit out, just this side of foaming at the mouth.

"So this never did have anything to do with vampires," Dana mused.

Blaise shot her a look. "Of course it did. What do you think she was blackmailing me over?"

"Wait," said, my little mental hamster jumping on her wheel as I took in his outfit again. "You mean, *you* are a vampire?"

"Oh, don't be so *Moonlight*. Of course I'm not. There is no such thing as a *real* vampire. But, once a month I played vampire at one of Sebastian's parties. Goldstein turned me on to them one night while I was in town signing some documents. He said they were a great way to unwind."

"And when Alexa started working here, she saw you at one," I finished.

He nodded. "Yes. Yes, she did."

"And she threatened to tell your wife about your dress-up fetish?"

Again he shot me a look like I was denser than a fruit cake. "No. She threatened to tell my wife that I slept with Becca after the party."

Mental forehead smack.

"So these are hook-up parties?" Dana asked.

Blaise nodded. "Nothing happens here, but if you want the fantasy to continue after hours, the girls are usually wiling to accommodate." He paused. "And I couldn't have Phoebe knowing that. She's a very sensitive woman. It would have killed her."

"So Alexa saw you here, watched you leave with her friend, then used that information to blackmail you," I said.

Blaise nodded. "Stupid whore thought I would actually pay her. Do you know how much money I've given her over the last three years?"

I shook my head. Not that I cared. But I realized that the longer we kept him talking the longer he wasn't shooting at us. I knew from many hours of *CSI* watching, that the bad guys never confessed unless they planned to get rid of the witnesses. The fact that he was spilling all didn't bode well for our future.

But it could buy us some time.

"Thousands," Blaise spit out, answering his own question. "Every month she came to us with her hand out, expecting me to empty my bank account. And then she had the nerve to ask for more to keep her mouth shut? Ha!" he laughed, though there was zero trace of humor in it. "No way." He paused, his demeanor changing. "My poor wife," he said, his voice low. "She is such a generous creature, and that Alexa just ran right over her. Exploited their relationship for everything she could. I couldn't let that happen. I couldn't let Alexa ruin us that way. I had to protect my wife."

"So you killed Alexa," I said, trying to keep him talking. I heard Marco moan at my feet, coming to. He shifted, and I noticed that Blaise hadn't had time to disarm him of his vampire hunting kit yet. Which might have come in handy if Blaise were a real vampire. As it was, gun trumped barbeque skewer any day.

Blaise nodded. "It was too easy, really. I followed her to Crush, then slipped a little something into her drink and waited. As soon as I saw her start to stumble, I jumped in, 'helping' her to the ladies' room," he said, doing an air quote with his free hand.

"Then you staged it to look like a vampire had killed her?" Dana asked, her eyes going to Marco and his bag. She noticed the same thing I did. She looked back up at me, and raised one eyebrow in a silent question.

Sadly, I couldn't think of any way to disarm a killer with Evian. I slowly shook my head in answer.

"I knew the vampire bite would keep the authorities guessing," Blaise continued, oblivious to our silent exchange. "There are enough shady things going on here, enough people with secrets, that the police could be chasing their tails for weeks trying to figure out which one of Sebastian's guests did it."

"And that's all you needed," I said, a light bulb going off as I remembered our last conversation with him. "Just some time. You were stalling until after the funeral, when you were going away with your wife." I paused. "You're not coming back are you?"

Blaise grinned, his face a spooky jack-o-lantern imitation in the pale flashlight beam. "No. I believe an extended vacation in the Bahamas is just what my wife and I need to reconnect."

"But what about Becca?" Dana asked. "Why kill her?"

"Because she had the nerve to pick up where Alexa left off," he spat out. "She said she knew I'd killed Alexa. That she'd seen me take her into the restroom at Crush, and she would tell the authorities if I didn't pay *her* off."

"What did you do?" I asked.

He grinned, obviously pleased with himself. "I told her to meet me at the next party. That I'd have her cash for her then. She did, I got her a drink, and then I told her I wasn't paying up. That she could go to the police if she wanted, but she had no proof, and I'd just tell them that she did it."

"But you knew she wasn't going to the police," I pointed out. "Because you spiked her drink."

He grinned. "I did. Two hours and she'd be showing her mortality."

"And you'd get away with everything."

"Right." He paused. "As long as no one else came nosing after the truth before I had a chance to get out of town."

I gulped. "Like us?"

"Exactly." He took a step toward us, his eyes narrowing. "Goldstein called me after you left his office yesterday. Asking all kinds of probing questions. I can't have people asking questions, Maddie," he said, pointing the gun at me. "Least of all, you."

Instinctively, I pushed back against the wall, but there was no place left for me to go.

And he knew it.

I looked down at Marco, who was awake now, his eyes blinking furiously, his mouth drawn into an "O" of surprise. If waking up in the dark had been disorienting, I could only imagine what waking up to a gun being pointed at you was like.

"So now you're going to kill us?" Dana squeaked out, making herself as small as I was attempting to do.

Blaise nodded, slowly. "I'm sorry. Really I am. I'm not a bad guy. But I can't have all of this coming out. My wife can't be hurt anymore. If she knew all of this, it would devastate her. You understand, right?"

What I understood was this guy was seriously unhinged.

I watched as he took one more step forward and aimed the gun at me. I froze, feeling time stand still as I watched him wrap his fingers around the trigger.

What happened next was a blur of motion.

I acted on pure instinct, doing what every urban girl has been trained to do in the event of an attack. I grabbed my purse, closed my eyes, and flung it at the bad guy, screaming as loudly as I could.

I heard the gun go off, the smell of burnt powder filling the room.

Then I heard Dana scream, "No!", and I opened my eyes to see her lunging at Blaise. He pointed the gun her way, but Dana had the element of surprise, tackling him from the side, wrapping both arms and legs around his middle in a wild piggyback motion.

Marco sprang into action, jumping up from the ground. "Demon from hell!" he shouted, reaching into his bag and throwing a vial of Evian at Blaise's face.

While it clearly didn't melt him with its holiness, it did stun him long enough for me to lunge forward on the floor, grabbing Blaise around the ankles and dropping him to the ground as Dana continued to wrestle him for the gun.

Another shot went off, pinging against the cement ceiling before it bounced down the corridor, causing us all to duck.

"Die, vampire scum!" Marco shouted, dipping into his bag and rushing at Blaise for another attack, this time stabbing him with a wooden skewer.

Though with Dana wrestling him on the ground, it was a little hard to aim directly at the heart.

"Ow, damn it," Blaise shouted, taking an over-sized toothpick to the arm.

I grabbed Marco's bag, digging for anything useful, and coming out with the spray can of tanner. I stood up, trying to take aim at Blaise as he struggled with Dana to maintain control of the gun. Dana's hours at the gym had given her muscles that were the envy of every other woman on the red carpet. But Blaise had her by a good hundred pounds, and it was clear she was losing.

"Die, you undead freak," Marco yelled, throwing another skewer, spear-style.

"Hey, watch it!" Dana shouted, taking a kabob spike to the thigh.

"Sorry," he said.

But it was just enough distraction to give Blaise the upper hand, wriggling from Dana's grasp and jumping to his feet.

"Don't move!" he shouted, panting as he straight-armed the gun at Dana.

She froze, doing a hands-up thing.

Then he swung it Marco's way. "And quit it with the poking!" he shouted at Marco.

Marco dropped the remaining skewers in his hand to the floor with a clatter.

"And, you…" Blaise said, spinning toward me.

But I was ready for him.

The second his eyes swung my way, I hit the button on the self-tanner, sending a stream of golden bronze colored chemicals right into his eyes.

Blaise screamed, both hands going to his face.

Dana lunged forward, doing her best kick-boxing move right to his groin.

Which cut his scream unceremoniously short, ending it in a crumpled sort of moan as Blaise doubled over, dropping the gun at his feet.

I quickly scooped it up and leveled it at him, my breath coming in hard pants.

"Don't you move," I yelled. "I am pregnant, I am pissed, and I have to pee. I *will* shoot you."

CHAPTER TWENTY-ONE

————

Ten minutes later, the foyer of Sebastian's house was crawling with police officers. And, oddly enough, my family members.

Apparently, Ramirez had gone home early that night, baring a plate of empanadas courtesy or his mother for yours truly. Only instead of me he'd found Mom and Mrs. R hard at work baby proofing again, having forgotten to install the wall straps on all of our furniture over three feet tall. While they strapped, Ramirez had wandered into the bathroom and seen the Fixodent and smoky-eyes make-up out. Being the brilliant detective he was, he'd put two and two together and quickly surmised that I was once again at Sebastian's house.

He, along with Mrs. R and Mom, who had insisted on coming along to make sure her practice grandbaby was okay, had arrived at the party just about the same time Blaise's gun had gone off. While no one might have heard the sound of us yelling, my husband knew the sound of a gunshot only too well. He'd called for backup, then run to the scene. Or at least as close to the scene as he could get.

As it turned out, our corridor was actually a secret passage built behind the library in Sebastian's house, one that Blaise later admitted to finding on a previous party visit. Ramirez had spent several minutes trying to figure out just where the sounds in the wall were coming from before employing Sebastian's help to unlock the secret door. (Which, by the way, was done by pulling out a Bram

Stoker book from the bookshelf. I totally should have looked there first.)

By the time Ramirez had finally made it to our private party, I had Blaise pinned to the ground with his own gun, Dana was nursing a sprained foot from the force of kicking Blaise's groin, and Marco was emptying the rest of the can of spray tan on a noticeably warmer colored Blaise.

Ramirez took one look at me and shook his head. "Oh, Lucy," he said, wrapping me in a tight embrace as his backup officers took Blaise into custody.

I returned it, only too glad to have the cavalry come to our aid.

"Oh, Maddie!" I heard behind him as my mom and Mrs. R pushed past the officers. She pounced, grabbing me in a hug so tight I feared she'd pop the baby right out of me.

"Oh, my darling, are you okay?" she said, pulling back to give me a once over.

I moved to nod, then, remembering my headache, thought better of it. "I'm fine," I reassured her instead.

"What happened?" Ramirez asked.

So I told him. Everything from our suspicions about Sebastian all the way to Blaise's confession and his threats at gunpoint.

"And you threw your purse at him? As the gun went off?" Ramirez asked, his voice going high.

I nodded slowly.

"Jesus," he muttered. "Maddie, you could have been killed." If I didn't know better, I'd say Ramirez's skin paled a shade.

"It was pure instinct," I protested. "It's a big bag. I thought maybe I could duck behind it."

The three of us looked down at my Santana bag on the ground. There was a neat, round, bullet hole in the center of it. I watched as a uniformed officer wearing a pair of latex gloves held it up. He peeked inside. Then he pulled out Baby-So-lifelike by its chubby vinyl hand. Right in the center of the doll's duckie-covered onesie was a neat, round hole.

Mom gasped and put a hand to her heart. "Oh, Maddie!"

I bit my lip. "Sorry, Mom. I swear I'll do better with a real one-" I started.

But she cut me off, going in for another boa-constrictor hug that nearly knocked the wind out of me. "I don't give a damn about that stupid doll. I'm just glad you're safe," she murmured into my hair.

I let out a deep sigh of relief.

* * *

The sun was just starting to come up as we left Sebastian's, Dana in an ambulance (though she protested that she was fine and ready to kick more butt if needed), Marco with a uniformed officer who promised to return all of his vampire hunting items as soon as they were logged out of evidence, and me with my husband. Who, once we got home, made me the biggest breakfast omelet in the world, brought me my fuzzy slippers, and tucked me into bed without even hinting at a yell over the fact that I'd nearly gotten our baby killed.

Again.

I wasn't sure how long I slept, but it felt like a million years. By the time I finally awoke the next morning I was stiff, but my headache had faded to a dull roar, which I took as a good sign. I slipped on a pink robe and padded into the kitchen where I put on a pot of coffee. Decaf. On the weak side. But that first sip tasted like heaven.

I took my cup into the spare room where I found Ramirez huddled over a mountain of paperwork. I felt just the tiniest twinge of guilt that I'd probably caused most of it.

"Knock, knock," I said from the doorway.

Ramirez spun around, a slow smile spreading across his face at the sight of me. "Hey, sleeping beauty. How you feeling?"

I shrugged. "Not bad." I held up my cup. "Getting better with every sip."

His grin widened. "I hope you made more."

I nodded, coming into the room. "I did, but it's decaf, so don't get too excited." I looked over his shoulder at the pile of papers. "This the paperwork on Blaise?" I asked.

Ramirez let out a long sigh. "Yeah. This guy was a real piece of work. We found the vial of Flunitrazepam in his place in Corona Del Mar. Looks like he bought it online from some place in Mexico. And turns out he'd already emptied his and his wife's bank accounts and had the money transferred to a place in the Caymans. Another week, and he would have been untraceable."

I resisted the urge to gloat over catching him. Mostly because until Blaise had pointed his gun at me, I'd had no idea he was involved.

"How's his wife taking it?" I asked, honestly feeling sorry for the woman.

Ramirez shrugged. "Not well. But I think she'll be okay."

"You know," I said, sipping at my coffee again. "There's one thing that's been bothering me. Why did Becca go to North Hollywood after the party that night? Why not just go home?"

Ramirez grinned at me. "You didn't know?"

"Know what?"

"See this is why you should leave the real investigating to the pros," he teased. "We're better at it."

I rolled my eyes. "Just tell me!"

"Okay, okay. Becca was sleeping with Darwin, Alexa's boyfriend. He lives in that building."

I scrunched my nose up. "Damn. Okay, you win, you got one on me." I paused, sipping. "So I guess Sebastian really didn't have anything to do with the murders after all?"

Ramirez shook his head. "No. In fact, he claims he had no idea the girls were going home with this guests, either."

I raised an eyebrow. "Do you believe him?"

Ramirez shrugged. "It's not a matter of what I believe, but what I can prove. And, frankly, I've already got my hands full here," he said, gesturing to the paperwork.

I nodded. "I guess so. But, if Sebastian was innocent, what was Becca's dress from the club doing in his bedroom?" Though even as I asked the question out loud, I felt the answer coming to me. Becca had been sleeping with Blaise, Goldstein, and Darwin. What did you want to bet she was playing hide the fangs with Sebastian as well?

"What dress?" Ramirez asked.

I shook my head. "Never mind. Not important."

"Hmm," he said, narrowing his eyes thoughtfully at me. Though, thankfully, he let it go.

I looked down at my cup and realized it was empty. "I'm gonna get a refill. You want one?" I asked.

"Please," Ramirez said, his eyes still watching me as I left the room.

I made my way into the kitchen and was just filling another cup when I felt Ramirez come up behind me, putting both arms around my middle. His lips went to my neck.

"You sure you're feeling okay," he whispered.

I grinned, trying not to giggle at the way his breath tickled. "Yeah. I'm fine."

"Hmmm, good." His lips moved lower, kissing along my shoulder. "Okay enough, say, to ditch the paperwork and go back to bed?"

I froze. "You mean… *bed*, bed?" I asked.

I felt Ramirez nod. "Uh huh."

I was two seconds away from ditching the robe, and my panties with it, but something made me pause. Instead of rushing for the bedroom, I spun around to face him.

"So, *now* you're in the mood?"

Ramirez grinned, his eyes a dark chocolate brown that told me he definitely was.

"Where exactly has this mood been the last four months?" I asked.

Ramirez paused, his eyes going just a shade lighter. "What do you mean?"

I wagged a finger at him. "Don't you play dumb with me, Jackson Wyoming Ramirez. You know what I mean. Tired, headaches, paperwork. You've been using every excuse in the book. What gives?"

He paused. Then looked down at the floor. "I just… well… I was kind of afraid of hurting the baby," he mumbled.

I did a forehead smack. A real one this time.

"Seriously?" I asked, blinking at him. "Honey, exactly how big do you think you are?"

Ramirez blinked at me. "What?"

I shook my head. "Forget it. Look, the fact is that it is a physical impossibility for you to get *anywhere* near the baby. In fact, my doctor said that sex is actually *good* for the baby. Not to mention me," I added.

Ramirez did some more blinking. "Oh." Then that grin slowly began to crease his cheeks again. "Well, that's good to know."

"Yeah, it is," I said. "It would also be good to know what suddenly has you ready to throw caution to the wind this morning. Was it the idea of almost losing me?" I asked, my voice going soft as I took a step toward him.

He grinned, his arms snaking around my middle again. But he shook his head. "As scary as that idea is, it's not exactly a turn on," he admitted.

"Okay, so then was it the sexy vampire outfit I wore last night?"

His eyes went a dark chocolate again, but he still shook his head.

"The coffee breath?" I fished.

"Nope."

"I give up, then. What did I do differently?" I asked.

He grinned wider. And maybe even blushed a little, if it was possible for Bad Cop to blush. "I don't know, Maddie. Something about seeing you hold that gun over Blaise. Being all kick ass like that. It was... kinda hot." he admitted.

I felt myself grin in response. "So 'Cagney' turns you on, huh?"

He frowned. "What?"

I shook my head. "Never mind. Just kiss me, you crazy cop."

And he did. Then Ramirez scooped me up (yes, all two tons of me) in his arms and made for the bedroom.

CHAPTER TWENTY-TWO

———

I crossed my legs, trying to ignore how badly I had to pee (for a change) as I waited patiently for the nurse to call me into the ultrasound technician's back room. I was pretty sure it was a form of torture that they'd told me to come with a full bladder, then made me wait twenty minutes until the tech could see me.

Ramirez shifted in his seat beside me, flipping the page on his copy of *Popular Mechanics*. I did the same, trying to focus on the *People* article in front of me and not my soon-to-be-exploding bladder.

Actually, it was a pretty interesting article, detailing the fall of Ava Martinez from super-stardom. Apparently her *Playboy* shoot had enraged more than just Dana. Posing nude was against her contract with the producers for the *Moonlight* movies, and once her spread had come out – where she was wearing a pair of fangs and nothing else – they'd dropped her option for the third movie.

Ricky's option, as Dana told me, however, had been renewed. Even though Crush had reopened and was doing so well that, as Dana had originally hoped, he hadn't needed to renew his contract for the third movie. But when the producers had come to him with a suggestion for his new leading lady, he hadn't been able to turn it down. Of course, Dana was now going to have to dye her hair black, but she and Ricky were going to be seeing a lot more of each other, both on and off the set. In preparation, Dana had started wearing her fangs twenty-four seven in order to lose her lisp.

"Springer?" a woman in scrubs called my name from the doorway.

"Oh thank God," I said, slamming my magazine down and fairly sprinting for the door.

I'll admit, not only was the full bottle of water the doctor had suggested I drink before driving here playing havoc with my bladder, but I was also just the teeniest bit nervous. This was the first time we'd really be able to see The Bump, not to mention find out whose gender predications were correct. I had an entire Amazon shopping cart full of pink baby clothes, just waiting for the word to hit "send".

I grabbed Ramirez's hand as we were led down a hallway that smelled like rubbing alcohol and Band-Aids, then into another room where I was instructed to lay down on a table. Luckily they didn't leave me alone long, a female technician appearing as soon as the woman in scrubs left. She quickly squirted icy-cold goop all over my belly and stuck a wand attached to a computer on it.

I watched nervously as images moved across the computer's screen. Mostly fuzzy. All black and white. None of them even slightly resembling a person as far as I could tell.

"Is that The Bump?" I asked. I paused. "I mean the baby?"

The technician nodded. "Uh huh."

"Is he supposed to look all fuzzy like that?" Ramirez asked, cocking his head to the side.

I grinned. I suddenly didn't feel like such a bad parent that I couldn't tell what was baby and what was screen static.

The technician smiled. "Yes. See, here you can see the hands, the feet, and this is its little rump."

"Can you tell if it's a girl or a boy?" I asked, silently chanting "pink, pink, pink" in my head.

She nodded. "We should be able to tell by now. Let me just see if I can get a better angle," she said, moving the wand around on my belly so that the image in the screen twisted sideways.

"Maybe just a little to the left here, and we should be able to tell… oh." The tech paused, her eyes squinting at the monitor.

"Oh?" I asked, butterflies suddenly taking hold in my stomach. "What does 'oh' mean?"

"It's just that… well, I'm not sure but… oh, my goodness"

"What?" I asked, nerves creeping into my voice. Oh god, what? Mom was right, I didn't know what to do with this parenthood. It wasn't even born yet, and already we were having an "oh my goodness" moment. It must have been the feta cheese I ate on my Greek salad before I took the pregnancy test. The soft cheese had done her in. Or maybe it was the lattes. Yes, I was a horrible person. I had snuck one when I'd been on caffeine-deprivation-headache day number three with no end in sight. Oh, God, my selfish latte binge had permanently disfigured my baby, I knew it.

"Is everything okay?" Ramirez asked, his voice amazingly calm compared to the mental breakdown I was silently having on the table.

"Well…" the technician frowned at the monitor again. "I don't know how no one has caught this yet. But I have some news for you."

I clenched my fists. I bit my lip. I steeled myself for the worst.

"News?" Ramirez asked, a hint of concern lacing his voice now, too.

And just when I was about to burst from fear (not to mention serious need to pee), the technician's concern smoothed out into a smile. "You're having a girl."

I let out a long breath, deflating my belly at least two inches in the process as visions of pink, frilly tutus, soft pink onesies, and teeny tiny pink shoes filled my brain.

"What was the 'oh my goodness' part?" Ramirez asked, ever the interrogator.

The technician looked from me to my husband, smiling even wider. "You're going to have a girl *and* a boy. It's twins!"

Oh boy.

ABOUT THE AUTHOR

Gemma Halliday is the author of the *High Heels Mysteries*, the *Hollywood Headlines Mysteries,* and the *Deadly Cool* series of young adult books. Gemma's books have received numerous awards, including a Golden Heart, a National Reader's Choice award and three RITA nominations. She currently lives in the San Francisco Bay Area where she is hard at work on several new projects.

To learn more about Gemma, visit her online at
www.GemmaHalliday.com